Voodoo really works!

Jessica tiptoed down the stairs in the dark and peered into the kitchen, where Steven was eating his usual late-night snack of a triple-decker bologna sandwich with ketchup and pickles. *He really is a pig,* she thought to herself.

Standing in the doorway, Jessica poked a thumbtack in the doll's stomach. Suddenly the real Steven grabbed his stomach.

She couldn't believe it! Her doll was working!

The real Steven doubled over in pain, making loud groaning noises. His disgusting sandwich fell out of his hand and onto the floor.

It worked! It worked! *Jessica thought to herself.* Voodoo really works!

SWEET VALLEY TWINS AND FRIENDS

Steven the Zombie

Written by
Jamie Suzanne

Created by
FRANCINE PASCAL

BANTAM BOOKS
NEW YORK · TORONTO · LONDON · SYDNEY · AUCKLAND

To Alice Elizabeth Wenk

RL 4, 008-012

STEVEN THE ZOMBIE

A Bantam Book / April 1994

*Sweet Valley High® and Sweet Valley Twins and Friends® are
registered trademarks of Francine Pascal*

Conceived by Francine Pascal

*Produced by Daniel Weiss Associates, Inc.
33 West 17th Street
New York, NY 10011*

Cover art by James Mathewuse

ISBN: 0-553-48104-5

Published simultaneously in the United States and Canada

*Bantam Books are published by Bantam Books, a division of Bantam
Doubleday Dell Publishing Group, Inc. Its trademark, consisting of the
words "Bantam Books" and the portrayal of a rooster, is Registered in
U.S. Patent and Trademark Office and in other countries. Marca
Registrada. Bantam Books, 1540 Broadway, New York, New York 10036.*

PRINTED IN THE UNITED STATES OF AMERICA

OPM   0 9 8 7 6 5 4 3 2 1

One

"Would ya'll be kind enough to save some of that meat loaf for little ol' me?" Jessica Wakefield asked her family in a heavy Southern accent at dinner on Sunday night.

The entire Wakefield family turned to look at Jessica in bewilderment.

"What are ya'll lookin' at? Do I have spinach in my teeth or somethin'?" Jessica asked.

"No, I think you have spinach in your brain," Jessica's older brother, Steven, teased.

"And I think you must have a volcano on your little ol' nose," Jessica teased back, still talking in a Southern accent. Jessica was referring to Steven's new pimple. She loved to tease him about his acne, since she knew how much he hated it.

"I think we could all do with a little less teasing

here," Mr. Wakefield said. "It's taking attention away from this delicious meal I made."

"Why, yes, it is delicious, I do declare." Jessica turned to her twin sister, Elizabeth. "Daahhlin', would you puh-leese pass me some of those bee-u-tiful mashed potatoes."

Suddenly Steven, Elizabeth, and Mr. and Mrs. Wakefield burst into hysterical laughter.

"What're y'all laughin' at?" Jessica asked, looking as though her feelings were hurt.

"Honey, I think we're laughing at your new Southern accent," Mrs. Wakefield said gently.

"Yeah, I think we're laughing at the fact that you sound like Dolly Parton," Steven said, holding his stomach because he was laughing so hard. "Did you have a brain exchange with some girl in Arkansas recently?"

Jessica gave her brother a withering stare. "For your information, although it's none of your business, Elizabeth and I have been studying about the Old South in social studies class. I've been reading this great book about life in New Orleans before the Civil War," Jessica said, finally dropping her accent.

Steven pretended that he was getting something out of his ear. "Excuse me, did I hear you correctly? I thought I just heard you say something about *reading*."

Elizabeth looked at her twin sister with a look that said, *Just ignore him, Jess.*

"Tell us what you've been learning about," Mr. Wakefield said.

"We've been learning all about slavery and how awful the slave owners were before the Civil War," Elizabeth said.

"I couldn't believe some of the horrible things we've read about and talked about in class," Jessica said.

"I know what you mean," Elizabeth agreed. "I always knew how terrible slavery was, but it is heartbreaking to read about the suffering of actual people. It makes it so real."

"I'm glad you girls are learning about this period in our country's history. It was a tragic era and one that every American should know about," Mr. Wakefield said.

Jessica nodded solemnly. "I know it is, but I have to admit that reading about all the gorgeous dresses the women wore back then and all the elegant balls they used to go to is more fun," Jessica said. Parties and clothes were two of Jessica's favorite subjects.

"Now, that sounds more like the Jessica we all know," Steven said. "I was beginning to worry about you for a minute there."

Jessica glared at Steven through narrowed eyes. He was always teasing her about being silly and never doing her schoolwork. She was getting really tired of it. She was sick of being thought of as the stupid twin.

Although both Jessica and Elizabeth had the same long, shiny blond hair, beautiful blue-green eyes, and dimples in their left cheeks, the similarities ended there. Elizabeth was the sister who did well in school and worked on the *Sixers*, the sixth-grade newspaper she helped start. She spent most of her time doing homework and reading. She wanted to be a writer when she grew up.

Jessica was more interested in boys and being popular than in being a good student. She loved to hang out with the Unicorns, the most popular and prettiest group of girls at Sweet Valley Middle School. Although Elizabeth was both pretty and popular enough to be a Unicorn herself, she thought the Unicorns were silly. Their meetings consisted mainly of conversations about boys, clothes, movie stars, fashion tips, and parties—stuff Elizabeth usually thought was boring.

But just because Jessica loved to talk about those things didn't mean she was dumb. Jessica decided she would show the world and especially her obnoxious brother that she could do well in school if she wanted to.

As she looked across the table at Steven stuffing his face with mashed potatoes, she sighed. Why was he always teasing her? Why was he always trying to make her feel stupid? *Sometimes I wish I didn't have a brother at all*, she thought.

Later that night, Jessica was reading in her book

about New Orleans. It was actually really fun to read. Especially when she got to the section called "Voodoo in Creole Society." She was fascinated by the detailed accounts of how people used voodoo dolls to torture their enemies.

She glanced up at the digital clock by her bed. It was two o'clock in the morning! She almost never stayed up that late, and if she did, it certainly wasn't to read!

She closed her book and kept the light on for a little while. She couldn't help feeling a little spooked from reading about all the voodoo rituals.

She tried to think peaceful thoughts, thoughts of the guys she had crushes on at school, and of floating on her back in the ocean. She glanced up at her Johnny Buck poster on the wall.

Suddenly she sat up straight in her bed. She felt her heart pounding in her chest. Was she seeing things, or had Johnny just given her a strange look? She rubbed her eyes and looked again. *This is really spooky*.

She jumped out of her bed and walked over to the poster to take a closer look. Wait a minute! Someone had taken a Magic Marker and turned her beloved Johnny Buck cross-eyed!

She stomped back to her bed. She didn't have to think too hard to figure out exactly who the culprit was: her no-good, teasing, awful brother Steven. He was always teasing her about how much she liked Johnny Buck. He was always saying what a bad actor and singer Johnny Buck was—just to annoy Jessica.

She was shaking with anger. This was the last straw. *You've gone too far this time*, Jessica thought to herself. *I'll make you sorry you ever picked up that Magic Marker, Steven Wakefield. My late-night reading will come in handy after all.* Jessica fell asleep with her book on top of her face, dreaming about what she would do to Steven.

"Settle down, class!" Mrs. Arnette was saying to her social studies class. It was Monday morning and the classroom was full of whispers as everyone got caught up on the weekend's activities. "We need to discuss class projects for this section. Presentations will be scheduled for next week. First of all, can I have volunteers to cook an authentic antebellum meal for the class?"

Before Elizabeth realized what was happening, Todd Wilkins, her sort-of boyfriend, raised his hand.

"Elizabeth and I would love to do it," Todd announced enthusiastically.

Elizabeth turned and glared at Todd, who was sitting at the desk next to hers. *We would?* Elizabeth thought to herself in disbelief. *That's news to me.* She knew she wasn't much of a cook, and she had a feeling Todd wasn't either.

"Todd, thanks a lot for signing me up without asking me first," Elizabeth whispered.

"Don't be mad. I knew if I asked, you'd probably say no, so I decided not to give you a choice," Todd whispered back, smiling.

When Todd smiled like that, it was impossible for Elizabeth to be mad at him. After all, this might be a good opportunity to spend some extra time with Todd. They were both so busy between her work on the newspaper and his basketball practices that they didn't get to see each other as much as she would have liked.

And the truth was, Todd had gone through a hard time recently. He'd gotten interested in writing, and his father had put a lot of pressure on him to quit the writing class and concentrate on basketball. Things were much better now, but still, Elizabeth didn't want to make Todd feel bad.

And besides, Elizabeth reasoned to herself, he was so talented at basketball and writing, he was probably great in the kitchen, too.

"OK," Elizabeth conceded a little while later as she and Todd walked to their lockers after class. "We'll do the meal together. But just tell me one thing. Have you ever cooked anything in your entire life before?"

Todd looked up at the ceiling, then down at his shoes. "Um . . . yeah . . . sure," he stammered.

"Look at me and tell me the absolute truth, Todd Wilkins."

"Well, let's see," he said, then paused. "One time on Mother's Day I brought my mom some cinnamon toast in bed," he said proudly.

"Cinnamon toast? That's not cooking," Elizabeth said, rolling her eyes playfully. "What else?"

Todd scratched his head and put his hand on his chin as if he were trying to figure out some difficult math problem.

"I know!" he exclaimed. "Last summer at the lake, I helped my dad cook hot dogs and burgers out on the grill. And not only that, I helped him cut potatoes for the potato salad."

Todd looked so proud that Elizabeth couldn't burst his bubble.

"Anyway, Elizabeth, how are you supposed to know what you're good at if you don't try things?" Todd asked.

"Yeah, yeah," Elizabeth said, smiling at him affectionately. "I guess there's no harm in trying."

I just hope this doesn't turn out to be a disaster, she couldn't help thinking as she shut her locker.

"What's everyone dressing up as for my party on Friday night?" Lila Fowler asked her friends in the Unicorn Club. They were all seated at the Unicorner, their usual table in the school cafeteria. Lila was one of the wealthiest girls in Sweet Valley, and her house was like a mansion, surrounded by gardens, a pool, and a tennis court. She loved to throw big, elaborate parties, like the antebellum party she was throwing on Friday night.

"I'm going as Scarlett O'Hara from the movie *Gone With the Wind*," Jessica announced.

"So am I!" Ellen Riteman, Tamara Chase, and Lila said in unison.

They all looked at one another and burst into laughter.

"Hey, that gives me a great idea," Janet Howell said. "I'm going to give a special prize to the Unicorn who I think is the best Scarlett O'Hara." Janet was an eighth-grader and the president of the Unicorns. She was also Lila's cousin. "I'll be an impartial judge, since I'm dressing up as Melanie, the sweet friend of Scarlett's in the movie."

"Isn't that a little out of character for you?" Ellen asked, giggling.

It was true that Janet could be loud and bossy, totally opposite from the sweet, naive character in the movie. But Jessica couldn't believe that Ellen would actually say that to Janet's face. None of the Unicorns wanted to be on Janet's bad side.

Janet dropped her tuna sandwich and glared at Ellen. "What exactly is that supposed to mean?"

"Well, you just . . . uh . . . seem more like the Scarlett type. You know, since you're so popular with the guys and everything," Ellen said quickly, realizing that she had said the wrong thing.

"Maybe there's a side of my personality you just don't know about," Janet said curtly. "I'm actually surprised that you're going as Scarlett, because *you* don't seem to have anything in common with *her.*"

Ellen's face turned bright red and she looked down at her plate of pasta salad in silence.

"I'm going as Harriet Beecher Stowe," Mandy Miller said, breaking the hush that had fallen over the table. "She was a preacher's daughter who wrote a book that helped to change people's opinions about slavery. I'm writing a biography about her for my social studies project. My mom's sewing my costume for me."

Mandy's always doing good and noble things like that, Jessica thought to herself. *She's kind of like Elizabeth in that way.* For one very brief moment, Jessica thought that maybe she should also go as somebody a little more important in history. The truth was, though, that Jessica had identified with Scarlett O'Hara ever since the first time she saw the movie. Especially the way Scarlett flirted and got the attention of all the guys. And Scarlett, like Jessica, managed to get herself out of some pretty serious scrapes.

Jessica decided that she would be the best Scarlett O'Hara in Sweet Valley. For one thing, she would love to get the approval of Janet, the most popular girl at Sweet Valley Middle School. And for another, she'd been so interested in the fancy dresses she'd been reading about in her book, she was thrilled to have a reason to get to wear one.

"What's everyone else doing for their social studies project?" Tamara asked.

"I'm throwing my antebellum party for my project," Lila said as she tossed her glossy brown hair over her shoulder.

"You honestly think The Hairnet will give you

credit for having a party?" Janet asked doubtfully as she took a bite of fruit salad. "The Hairnet" was a nickname for Mrs. Arnette, since she wore a hairnet over her bun every day.

"Of course," Lila answered defensively. "I've had to study up on different kinds of foods and dances and decorations from that period of time. I probably know more about the antebellum South than anyone in class."

"Well, I'm doing a presentation about the movie stars," Ellen said.

All the Unicorns looked at one another and started laughing.

"Ellen, there weren't any movie stars back then. There weren't even any movies," Janet said.

"I know that," Ellen said, obviously annoyed about being laughed at. "I'm going to talk about the movie stars who were in *Gone With the Wind*. You know—like Vivian Leigh and Clark Gable."

"The Hairnet must have changed a lot since I had that class in sixth grade," Janet said. "I don't think we could have gotten away with doing projects like that in my day."

"What about you, Jessica? What are you doing for your social studies project?" Tamara asked.

Jessica had been absorbed in her thoughts about her Scarlett dress and hadn't been following the conversation too closely.

"I'm sorry, what did you ask?" Jessica asked, taking the last bite of hamburger.

"What's your social studies project?" Tamara asked again.

Until that moment, Jessica hadn't really thought about what to do for her project. Suddenly an idea popped into her head. *If I'm going to be doing voodoo on Steven anyway, I might as well do it for my project and get credit.*

"My project is very, very special," Jessica said in an almost-whisper. Her eyes narrowed. She looked over her shoulder, then leaned in toward the group. All the Unicorns leaned in to share her dark secret. "I can't say exactly what it is, but I *will* say that it has something to do with witchcraft. I can guarantee that my presentation will be the best and scariest project anyone in the history of Sweet Valley Middle School has ever seen."

Two

After school on Monday, Elizabeth and Amy Sutton, Elizabeth's best friend after Jessica, stopped by the day-care center that was attached to Sweet Valley's homeless shelter. Elizabeth liked to spend afternoons there when she had free time, playing with kids, reading them books, or painting pictures with them.

This particular afternoon, Elizabeth had been playing checkers with an eight-year-old boy named Benjamin, who walked with a cane.

"What do you want to be when you grow up?" Elizabeth asked him after he beat her for the third time.

"I want to be an astronaut or a baseball player," he said excitedly.

"Those are great things to be," Elizabeth said.

"Yeah, but I guess that's pretty impossible with my leg problem," Benjamin added sadly.

"What's wrong with it?" Elizabeth asked gently.

"Nobody really knows," Benjamin responded. "I've seen lots and lots of doctors, but nobody knows what the matter is. They think it might be some kind of bone disease. They say it will probably get worse as I get older." Benjamin was putting all the checkers away into a paper bag.

"Well, what are the symptoms?" Elizabeth asked.

"I have pains in my leg and nothing makes them go away," Benjamin replied.

"What about you?" Benjamin asked, changing the subject. "What do you want to be when you grow up?"

"I'm going to be a writer," Elizabeth said. She looked into his big, hopeful blue eyes and then at the cane leaning against his chair. She wished there were some way this little boy's dreams to be an astronaut or a baseball player could come true.

"I feel awful for Benjamin," Elizabeth said to Amy as they walked home. "It's just so sad for somebody so young not to be able to run around like other kids."

"I know," Amy agreed. "It really makes you realize how lucky we are."

"I take so much for granted," Elizabeth said, looking down at her legs as she walked. "Like walking, for example. Did you ever stop to think about the fact that you have two healthy legs that you can walk with?"

"No, actually," Amy said, laughing. "But you're right, Elizabeth. It really does make you think about everything in a different way when you meet somebody like Benjamin.

Suddenly Elizabeth had an urge to be a little kid again. "I'll race you to the end of the block," she said.

"You're on! On your mark, get set, go!" Amy commanded.

The two girls ran as fast as they could then fell down on the grass and broke into giggles.

"I won!" Elizabeth declared gleefully.

"Jess, aren't you a little old to be playing with dolls?" Elizabeth asked as she walked into her sister's room later that afternoon.

Jessica was holding one of Steven's old G.I. Joe dolls. She had made a little brown wig for it and had dressed the doll in a rough imitation of jeans and a blue oxford shirt. Elizabeth saw Steven's cut-up oxford shirt on the bed and gasped.

"That's Steven's lucky shirt! He's going to kill you!" Elizabeth exclaimed. She shot her sister a suspicious look. "What are you up to, Jess?" Elizabeth could always tell when her twin was up to some new scheme. Jessica got a little sparkle in her eye that only her sister noticed.

"First of all, keep your voice down," Jessica whispered. She walked over to her door, peered into the hallway, shut the door, then tiptoed back over to her bed.

"Do you swear you won't tell one single living human being what I am about to tell you?"

"I swear."

"Cross your heart and hope to die? Stick a needle in your eye?"

"Cross my heart."

"Hold up your hands so I know you're not crossing your fingers," Jessica commanded.

Elizabeth held up her hands, but she crossed her toes. She sometimes did that as a precaution when Jessica was about to divulge one of her grand plans. She never knew if she would have to bail her sister out of some mess, and it was easier when she could tell the truth. She knew it wasn't exactly being honest, but she figured it was for Jessica's own good.

"OK, you know how I've been reading about the Old South for social studies class?" Jessica said excitedly.

"I've been reading about it, too, you know. We *are* in the same class after all," Elizabeth said, starting to get exasperated.

"Right. Well, I've been reading a lot about voodoo. And I've made a voodoo doll of Steven to get back at him for ruining my Johnny Buck poster. Look at this," Jessica said, holding up the Steven doll. "Isn't this just the spitting image of our obnoxious brother?"

Elizabeth couldn't help laughing.

"I guess it does look an awful lot like Steven," she said between giggles.

"This will look even more like him." Jessica grabbed a red pen from her desk and proceeded to draw little pimples on the doll's face.

"What exactly are you planning on doing with that doll?" Elizabeth asked.

"Nothing too mean. Only a few little painful pokes and tugs. Just enough to make him suffer," Jessica said with a devilish smile.

"You don't honestly believe this stuff do you?" Elizabeth asked, although she didn't really want to know the answer.

"As a matter of fact, I *do* believe this stuff," Jessica said defensively. "Besides, you know I have special psychic powers."

Jessica had always believed she was psychic. In fact, one time she and Elizabeth were on television because of these powers she thought she had. They were supposed to be in a school talent show, but Elizabeth didn't show up because she was locked inside a building. Jessica led the TV cameras to Elizabeth, and the rescue was captured on TV. Elizabeth thought it was more a matter of common sense than psychic powers, but she couldn't convince Jessica of that.

"There's no scientific proof that voodoo works, Jess."

"Is there any scientific proof that it doesn't

work?" Jessica demanded, annoyed by Elizabeth's predictable, practical reaction.

Elizabeth knew her sister well enough to know when her mind was set about something. Jessica was going to believe in voodoo no matter what Elizabeth said.

Jessica couldn't wait for Elizabeth to leave her room so she could try out her first voodoo experiment. She held up the doll in one hand and a hat pin in the other. "Sorry, Steven, but all is fair in love and war. I love Johnny Buck, and I'm at war with you."

Jessica poked the doll in the right foot then listened at the wall that separated her room from Steven's for a cry of pain. Nothing.

She ran down the hall and into Steven's room, only to find him sitting calmly on his bed, reading a book.

"Didn't you see the 'knock before entering' sign on the door?" Steven asked, annoyed.

Jessica just stood there silently, unable to think of anything to say.

"So what do you want?" he asked, becoming even more irritated.

"Uh . . . uh . . ." Jessica stammered. She looked around his messy, cluttered room and grabbed the first thing that caught her eye—a big red umbrella.

"This is what I needed. Sorry to disturb you," Jessica said, walking out of the room.

"Excuse me, Miss Marshmallow-for-Brains, but

there's not one cloud in the sky, it hasn't rained in a month, and it probably won't rain for another month."

Jessica hated the stupid things Steven called her. But instead of thinking of something insulting to call him, she remembered her voodoo doll and stayed calm.

"You're probably right, Steven. But sometimes the weather can be so unpredictable and I just like to be prepared." With that, Jessica ran as quickly as she could out the door.

Elizabeth sat on her bed before dinner that evening surrounded by dozens of cookbooks. She never realized just how many different kinds of cookbooks there were, or how many her parents owned.

She and Todd had agreed that she would be in charge of actually choosing the recipes for the meal that they would cook together. But the only thing she knew about Southern cooking was fried chicken. Her goal was to find the simplest menu, one that it would be impossible to mess up. The truth was, she didn't want to admit to Todd that she wasn't really very much of a cook herself. She'd had more than one fiasco when she'd attempted to bake cookies and cakes in the past. And whenever it was her turn to make the family dinner, she usually just made a big tuna fish salad.

After reading through all the books, Elizabeth

wrote down her final menu: hush puppies, corn bread, black-eyed peas, peach cobbler, and something called fish gumbo, which she'd never heard of.

This stuff sounds delicious, and it seems pretty easy to make, Elizabeth thought. *Maybe we'll make a terrific meal after all. How hard can it be?*

Jessica was in her room, sitting on the floor looking through one of the books about the Old South that Elizabeth had taken out from the library. The book had great pictures of the kinds of dresses wealthy Southern women used to wear. She saw so many dresses that she loved, she didn't know how she would decide which style to wear to Lila's party. She was sure she wanted one that came in really narrow at the waist and had a full skirt. One of the pictures showed a diagram of all the layers women wore. Jessica couldn't believe it. Ten petticoats? *How did women walk with all that stuff?* she wondered.

The only thing was, where did you find one of these dresses? Jessica didn't think there was a store in Sweet Valley that sold antebellum fashions. She could always see if her mom would be willing to sew one for her. But she was pretty sure that something on that scale would be a little more complicated than the things her mother was used to sewing.

No matter what, I will win the Best Scarlett prize, Jessica thought. She loved a challenge, and this one was right up her alley.

*   *   *

"Take a picture—it lasts longer," Steven said to Jessica that night at the dinner table.

Jessica was watching Steven's every move, looking for signs that her voodoo doll was working.

"I'm just concerned about your health. How are you feeling? Any aches or pains?" Jessica asked sweetly.

Elizabeth had to cover her face with her napkin to hide her giggles. "Ouch!" she exclaimed as Jessica kicked her under the table.

"I guess it's Elizabeth who's feeling the aches and pains around here," Steven said. "What's with you?"

"I just felt a little growing pain in my leg. That's all," Elizabeth lied.

"Speaking of legs," Elizabeth continued, trying to change the subject, "I met the sweetest kid today at the day-care center. His name is Benjamin and he has to walk with a cane. Nobody really knows what's wrong with him. He has terrible pain all the time in his right leg. It's so sad because he's only eight and he can't run around and play with the other kids."

"That's just horrible," Mrs. Wakefield said. "We should all realize how lucky we are to be healthy."

"That's exactly what I was thinking today. I just take things like the ability to walk for granted," Elizabeth said.

"Hey, I've got an idea. Why don't we have him over here for dinner some night?" Mr. Wakefield suggested.

"That would be great!" Elizabeth said excitedly. "I'll go call Mrs. Weissman at the day-care center and see if she can arrange with his mom a night for him to come over."

Jessica had been listening to the discussion about Benjamin halfheartedly until a thought came into her head. *If voodoo can be used to cause pain, why can't it be used to take pain away?*

Jessica was lying on her bed after dinner, wondering why her voodoo wasn't working yet. She decided to make the doll look even more like Steven. That would probably help.

She took some construction paper and carefully made a miniature blue baseball cap like the one Steven always wore. And she fastened a little sign on the front of the doll's shirt that said, "My name is Steven."

Maybe she should try a little more voodoo before going to bed, Jessica thought. She had just read the play *Macbeth* by William Shakespeare in her English class. The play had some witches in it, so she decided to use one of their chants and see if that would get her special powers going.

"Double, double toil and trouble; fire burn and cauldron bubble. Let my brother feel the pain, which I inflict into his vein."

On her way out of the room, she caught a glimpse of herself in the mirror and felt a sudden chill rush through her body. For a moment, she was worried she detected a witch wart growing on her nose. *I hope I don't start looking like a witch*, Jessica thought nervously.

Jessica tiptoed down the stairs in the dark and peered into the kitchen, where Steven was eating his usual late-night snack of a triple-decker bologna sandwich with ketchup and pickles. *He really is a pig*, she thought to herself.

Standing in the doorway, Jessica poked a thumbtack in the doll's stomach. Suddenly the real Steven grabbed his stomach. She couldn't believe it! Her doll was working!

The real Steven doubled over in pain, making loud, groaning noises. His disgusting sandwich fell out of his hand and onto the floor.

It worked! It worked! Jessica thought to herself. *Voodoo really works!*

Three

"Steven, you've barely touched your french toast. What's the matter? You love french toast," Mrs. Wakefield said at the breakfast table on Tuesday morning.

"I'm kind of bummed out about this stupid math test I have today. This new stuff we've been doing is really intense. And I guess I didn't sleep that well last night," Steven said as he moved the french toast around with his fork.

"Cheer up. You always do well in math," Mrs. Wakefield said reassuringly.

Jessica was hiding her Steven doll in her lap during breakfast and couldn't resist the opportunity to have a little fun. When she thought nobody was looking, she tickled the doll behind the knees, which she knew was Steven's most ticklish spot.

Suddenly Steven started laughing uncontrollably.

"My goodness," Mr. Wakefield said, peering
over his newspaper. "You certainly took your
mother's advice to the extreme." He looked at his
wife. "You're very persuasive, honey. You'll have to
tell me your trick, so I'll know how to get him
away from the TV set the next time I need him to
take out the trash."

"This is a surprise to me. I never knew I had so
much influence on you, Steven," Mrs. Wakefield said.

Jessica couldn't stop herself from laughing because of her little secret, and Elizabeth could never
keep herself from laughing whenever Jessica was
cracking up. The laughter was contagious, and
soon all five Wakefields were laughing.

"You must have put something in the french
toast, Mom," Elizabeth said between giggles.

"Whatever it is, I hope we'll have some more tomorrow morning," Mr. Wakefield said.

"Wait! That's salt, not sugar!" Elizabeth yelled to
Todd.

Elizabeth and Todd had decided to get together
at Todd's house after school that day and practice
cooking together. After two hours they were on
their third round of corn bread. They had thrown
the first two batches out. The first one had been so
hard, Elizabeth had almost lost a tooth trying to
bite into it. The second batch had been totally

burned on the bottom. And even though they were making it together, Elizabeth couldn't help feeling that both fiascoes were Todd's fault.

"Look, Elizabeth, if you keep watching me so closely, I'm never going to get this right. Why don't you go do some homework in the living room while I stay here and finish this batch? You know what they say about too many cooks in the kitchen," Todd said, trying not to sound irritated.

Elizabeth looked at Todd. He had flour all over him. *He really is trying hard to do this right*, she thought. Still, there was no way she could let him stay in there by himself. There was no telling what might happen. He might burn the house down.

"Why don't *I* stay in the kitchen and *you* go do some homework in the living room?" Elizabeth offered. "I really don't mind, and I don't have all that much homework today anyway."

"I don't have much homework either. I guess we both should just stay here and get it right," Todd said.

Twenty minutes later the last batch was ready. When they took the corn bread out of the oven, it actually looked the way it was supposed to.

"Hey, you should take this home to your family for dinner tonight and see what they think," Todd said excitedly. "Call me after dinner and tell me how they liked it."

"That's a great idea," Elizabeth lied. She was actually afraid that it might not taste as good as it looked, but she didn't want to tell Todd that. He looked so proud and happy she just couldn't bear to rain on his parade.

Jessica was lounging happily on the couch in the family room after school that afternoon, watching her favorite soap opera. She had a tall glass of lemonade and a bowl of popcorn.

The two stars of the show were about to see each other after a long, tragic separation, and Jessica had been waiting for weeks for them to get back together.

Suddenly Steven bounded into the room, grabbed the remote control from the coffee table, and flipped the channel to a basketball game.

She didn't yell at Steven as she normally did. Instead, she ran upstairs to her room and grabbed her voodoo doll and a safety pin. She went back to the family room, sat back down on the couch, and hid the doll under a blanket.

"Steven, would you like some popcorn?" she asked sweetly.

"Sure," Steven said, looking slightly puzzled by Jessica's unusually kind offer.

As Steven walked back to his chair carrying the bowl of popcorn, Jessica poked the doll's feet with the pin. To Jessica's amazement, Steven started hopping around the room, howling. The bowl flew out of his hands and the floor was covered with popcorn.

"Mom's gonna kill me," Steven said once he stopped jumping around.

"The vacuum's in the hall closet," Jessica said with the same sweet voice.

As soon as Steven left the room, Jessica grabbed the remote control and put her soap opera back on. Luckily, the show was just coming back from a commercial, and she got to see the couple fall into each other's arms. *This voodoo stuff certainly comes in handy*, she thought.

"It was so nice of you to have me over for dinner," Benjamin said to the Wakefield family as they were sitting down at the table.

"Well, we're just so happy to have you here, Benjamin. It's really a treat for us," Mrs. Wakefield said as she served him lasagna and salad.

"This meal's going to be about a hundred zillion times better than the ones we have at the center. I can tell already," Benjamin said excitedly.

"We have another special treat tonight. Elizabeth made this beautiful corn bread," Mr. Wakefield said as he put a big piece on his plate.

"I can't take all the credit," Elizabeth said. "Todd and I made it together."

"Elizabeth tells me you're an ace checkers player," Steven said to Benjamin. "How about playing a game with me after dinner?"

"That would be great! I don't get much competition at the center. Not one kid there has beaten me," Benjamin said proudly.

Jessica pushed the salad around on her plate thoughtfully. "Benjamin, Elizabeth also told us about the pain you have in your right leg. Where exactly do you feel it?" she asked.

"Gee, Jessica, I didn't know you'd become a doctor," Steven teased.

"Right here," Benjamin said, moving his leg out from under the table and pointing to a spot just below his knee.

"Hmmm," Jessica said. "And when do you usually feel the pain?"

"You don't have to answer her. She can be a little nosy sometimes," Elizabeth said to Benjamin. She gave Jessica a look that Jessica chose to ignore.

"That's OK. I don't mind talking about it. I'm so used to talking to different doctors and nurses all the time," Benjamin said. "I guess it usually feels worst when I'm about to go to sleep."

"And what time is that?" Jessica asked.

"Around eight-thirty," Benjamin said.

"Well, I for one am going to try this delicious-looking corn bread," Mrs. Wakefield said.

"Why doesn't everyone try it?" Mr. Wakefield suggested.

A minute later everyone at the table was gagging and grabbing their water. The corn bread was incredibly salty and so chewy it was like eating chewing gum. One at a time, everyone politely spat it back into their napkin.

"Did you put glue in there?" Steven gasped.

Elizabeth just shook her head, mortified. "I don't know what happened," she moaned. "I watched everything Todd put in there so closely."

At that moment the phone rang.

"I'll get it," Jessica said as she leapt up from the table.

"Lizzie, it's Todd!" Jessica said loudly.

"Tell him I'm not here," Elizabeth whispered urgently.

"I already told him you were," Jessica whispered back.

Reluctantly, Elizabeth stepped into the kitchen and took the phone from Jessica. "Hello," she murmured into the receiver.

". . . Uh, yeah, they loved it. . . . Oh, absolutely. It turned out great. I gotta go. 'Bye!" Elizabeth hung up the phone abruptly. She hated lying more than anything, but she couldn't stand the idea of upsetting Todd either.

"Maybe you should consider getting a new cooking partner," Steven said when she'd sat back down at the table. "Next time he's over here I think I'll tell him he should stick to the basketball court and stay away from the kitchen."

Elizabeth glared at him. "You better not, Steven, or I'll—"

"Relax," Steven interrupted. "I won't say anything to him. But seriously, judging by tonight's sample, I don't think cooking is his thing. Did you say you're getting graded on this project?"

"Steven, stop it. I think Todd deserves a second chance," Mr. Wakefield said as he poured more glasses of iced tea and water all around the table. "Cooking's like painting or playing basketball or just about anything else in life. It only takes a little practice."

"I agree," Elizabeth said, defending Todd. "All Todd needs is a little practice."

She looked down at the soggy piece of corn bread on her plate. *At least I hope that's all he needs*, she added to herself.

Four

"I've found the most perfect Scarlett dress," Lila announced at Booster practice in the gymnasium Wednesday afternoon. The Boosters were Sweet Valley Middle School's cheering and baton squad, which comprised mainly Unicorns except for Amy Sutton and Winston Egbert.

"Where'd you find it?" Tamara asked as she stood up from a cartwheel.

"It's from a museum shop in New York. It just came in the mail last night, and it fits me perfectly," Lila said, leaning against the wall to stretch her calf muscles.

Jessica was trying to practice a difficult new baton twirl, but she was finding it hard to concentrate. Lila could be such a show-off sometimes. It wasn't only that Jessica was worried about not having a dress for the party—she just thought it wasn't nice for Lila to brag like that. Not everyone could afford to send away to New York for an expensive dress. Lila's bragging made Jessica even more determined to win the Best Scarlett competition.

"I found a gorgeous dress in the costume shop downtown," Ellen said as she did the splits on the floor. "It was the only one they had in the right style. I was so lucky I got there before anyone else grabbed it."

"What does it look like?" Tamara asked.

"It's white with green trim and has a really narrow waist and a super full skirt. My mom says I look exactly like Scarlett in it," Ellen bragged.

Jessica dropped her baton. *That's my dream dress she's describing*, Jessica thought to herself worriedly.

"What about you, Jessica?" Janet asked. "Do you have your Scarlett dress yet?"

"Of course I do," Jessica lied.

"Tell us about it," Janet pressed.

"It's absolutely gorgeous. I don't want to tell you about it, though, because I want it to be a surprise," Jessica said as she picked up her baton.

"Have you thought of what prize you're giving the best Scarlett yet?" Mandy asked.

"Yes, I have, as a matter of fact," Janet said with her usual air of authority. "The winner gets to be the acting president of the Unicorns while I'm in Aspen with my family for a week."

Jessica had always imagined herself becoming the president of the Unicorns someday. This would be a perfect opportunity to try the job out before she could become the actual president, which probably wouldn't be for a year or two, since she was only in sixth grade.

She watched Lila fiddling with her pom-poms. She would absolutely hate it if somebody else got the job instead of her—especially if it was Lila. Even though Lila was her best friend after Elizabeth, she was always competing with Jessica. Also, Janet and Lila were first cousins, so Janet often gave her cousin preferential treatment.

"Does anybody know what any of the guys are dressing up as?" Tamara asked.

"I think most of them are going as Rhett Butler," Lila said. "I spread the word around that the best Rhett Butler gets the first dance with me."

Jessica looked across the gym at her friend and rolled her eyes. How typical of Lila to assume that every guy would be dying to have the first dance with her. It was true that Lila was beautiful, with her straight brown hair and big brown eyes, but there were a lot of guys who would want to dance with Jessica, too.

"What kind of dancing are you going to have?" Ellen asked.

"My dad hired a professional fiddler and caller to lead everyone in square dancing," Lila said boastfully.

"Oh, goody! I love square dancing," Amy said as she threw her baton in the air.

"*Square* dancing?" Jessica, Mandy, Ellen, and Janet all said in disbelief.

"That's really pretty babyish, isn't it?" Janet asked, making a face as if she'd just eaten something that tasted sour. "I mean, maybe you sixth graders are still square dancing, but some of us have moved on to more exciting things."

Jessica couldn't help enjoying Janet's put-down. Lila, like Jessica and all the other Unicorns, considered herself to be very mature. Being called "babyish," especially by Janet, was about the worst insult she could think of.

"Well, there's going to be other kinds of dancing, too, of course," Lila said defensively. "Square dancing is just one of the kinds."

"That's a relief," Janet said.

"Yeah, I'd like to see Bruce Patman square dancing," Jessica said, laughing. Bruce Patman was a seventh grader and one of the wealthiest and handsomest boys at Sweet Valley Middle School. Jessica had had a very short romance with him and decided that he was also one of the most obnoxious and arrogant guys at school.

Lila shot a look of annoyance across the room at Jessica, who refused to acknowledge it. Jessica couldn't resist the temptation to jump on the bandwagon with Janet and tease Lila. "I'm sure the nerdy chess club members will enjoy the square dancing. That's about their speed," Jessica added. Now everyone was laughing. Everyone except Lila.

When Jessica got home that afternoon she saw Steven playing a game of checkers in the living room with Benjamin. Benjamin was laughing hysterically.

"What's so funny?" she asked.

"I just beat Steven for the fifth time!" Benjamin said, clapping his hands.

"That's terrific!" Jessica said. Steven was an ace checkers player and Jessica was sure he must have let Benjamin beat him. *That's nice of Steven to let him win*, she thought to herself. *I guess even the most obnoxious people in the world are capable of a kind act every now and then.*

Jessica looked at Benjamin's smiling face and then down at the cane leaning against his chair. For a minute she had forgotten his disability and just saw him as a healthy, happy boy.

"How's your leg been lately?" Jessica asked with a concerned expression.

"Here's Dr. Wakefield again, ladies and gentlemen," Steven said, using his television announcer's voice.

He's back to his obnoxious self, Jessica thought with a sigh.

"Actually, it's been pretty bad lately. Last night I could barely sleep at all," Benjamin said.

"Isn't there any kind of medicine that helps take the pain away?" Jessica asked.

"The doctor gave me something new to try, but it doesn't seem to be working yet. I'm so sick of being tired all the time from not sleeping at night," Benjamin said.

"What does Dr. Wakefield prescribe?" Steven teased.

Jessica ignored her brother. "I have a feeling your pain is going to go away soon," she said. *And I have a feeling you're about to feel some new pain soon, Steven,* she thought to herself.

"I sure hope you're right," Benjamin said, smiling up at her.

"As a matter of fact, I sometimes have strong feelings about things like this and I'm usually right," Jessica said.

"My sister thinks she's a psychic or something," Steven whispered loudly to Benjamin as Jessica left the room.

Jessica smiled to herself. Little did Steven know.

Jessica headed upstairs to the attic, where she kept her old dollhouse and took out one of the little dolls. She found some pieces of fabric, too.

Back in her room, she carefully cut a little white shirt out of one piece of fabric and a pair of jeans from the other. She dressed the doll up to look just like Benjamin. Then she thought of the perfect final touch. She cut off a little piece of her own blond hair and glued it on the doll's head.

A few minutes later she crept down to the

kitchen, relieved that no one was in there. She quickly made a special potion out of rose petals, perfume, crushed vitamin C, milk, and honey. She boiled it all together on the stove, then brought it upstairs in a bowl to her room. She spread the potion all over the doll's right leg with her lucky rabbit's foot.

"Double, double toil and trouble; Fire burn and cauldron bubble. Take away this boy's pain, so he won't ever need a cane," she whispered.

She wasn't sure where to put the doll, so she built him a miniature house out of a shoe box. She even included a tiny television set she'd made out of cardboard. Jessica couldn't remember the last time she spent so much time on a project like this. *This voodoo stuff sure takes a lot of work and concentration*, she thought.

Just as she was putting on the final touches, Elizabeth walked into the room. Jessica jumped in surprise.

"Please knock next time. You scared me to death," Jessica said. "I thought you were Steven."

Elizabeth just stood there silently, staring at the doll in Jessica's hand.

"What are you looking at?" Jessica asked. She looked down at the doll then back at Elizabeth. "Oh, this. OK, go shut my door and I'll explain it to you."

Elizabeth shut the door and then sat down on Jessica's bed. "Just tell me that you haven't gone completely crazy, OK? I mean, it's fine to be playing with dolls if you want, I guess, but it is kind of weird." Elizabeth pointed to the little dollhouse that Jessica built. "And what is *this*?"

"OK, you know how Benjamin has that horrible pain in his leg?" Jessica asked.

"Yes, of course I do. I'm the one who told *you* about it," Elizabeth said.

"Right. Well, I've come up with a way to make his pain go away," Jessica said, beaming.

Elizabeth looked at her sister with both amusement and concern. She was used to her sister's bizarre plans and schemes. This one was starting to sound really strange, though.

"Let me guess. You've found a doctor who has a medically proven cure," Elizabeth said, knowing full well that wasn't the case.

"No," Jessica said.

"You read a magazine article about diseases like Benjamin's and how they've been treated in some far-off tropical climate," Elizabeth continued.

"Nope," Jessica said, about to burst from keeping in her secret.

"You've been taking medical classes on the side, and now you're a doctor like the kid on that TV show," Elizabeth said.

Jessica burst out laughing. "No. No, and no."

"OK, what? Tell me."

Jessica took a deep breath and handed the little Benjamin doll to Elizabeth. "Now, I know what you're going to say, but don't say it. Anything negative could hurt the chances of this working," Jessica said in a serious tone.

"Of what working?" Elizabeth had a skeptical look on her face.

"First of all, wipe that expression off your face," Jessica commanded.

Elizabeth tried to make a serious expression, but that only made her laugh more.

"If you're going to laugh, then I won't tell you."

"Just get on with it," Elizabeth said.

"OK, the doll you're holding is Benjamin."

Elizabeth looked at the little doll and started laughing harder than ever.

"Out of my room!" Jessica said sternly. "That's it. This is serious and you're going to ruin everything if you keep laughing." Jessica was getting really upset now.

"OK, I promise not to laugh." Elizabeth took a deep breath and tried to pull herself together. "You were saying that this is Benjamin."

"Right. It's a healing doll. It works the same way as a voodoo doll, except that it's used to make people feel better instead of hurting them," Jessica said matter-of-factly.

"And you're going to make the real Benjamin's leg all better with this doll," Elizabeth said. She was trying with all her might not to laugh. She knew when Jessica was on the verge of really getting mad, and she didn't want to cause a scene.

"Exactly. Now you're catching on," Jessica said.

"And how exactly do you plan on achieving this?" Elizabeth asked, her lips twitching.

"I can't tell you right now because it might ruin the process. And please, don't think any doubtful thoughts about it or it won't work."

"It's a deal. I won't think any negative or doubtful thoughts," Elizabeth said to humor her twin.

"And most important, don't under any circumstances tell what I've just told you to any living, breathing person. Do you promise?"

"I promise," Elizabeth said, holding up her hands to show that no fingers were crossed. Once again, she crossed her toes. "Just tell me one more thing. What's the deal with this little shoe box?"

"That's Benjamin's house. I wanted him to have a comfortable place to stay while he's healing."

"I see. Well, I gotta go do some studying." Elizabeth left the room as fast as she could before she broke into uncontrollable giggles.

"Where's Steven?" Jessica asked when she saw that Steven's chair was empty at dinner that night.

"He said he was feeling nauseous so he was going to skip dinner and go right to bed," Mrs. Wakefield said.

"Nauseous? Hmmm." Jessica thought immediately of how she'd spun the Steven doll in circles before coming down to dinner. "That's pretty unusual for him. Normally, he's a walking trash compactor," she commented. "I can't remember the last time he skipped a meal."

"I'm starting to worry about him. He hasn't really been himself lately," Mrs. Wakefield said.

"He has been behaving a little strangely, hasn't he?" Mr. Wakefield said. "I wonder if he's coming down with something."

Jessica couldn't help smiling. *He sure has come down with something,* she thought triumphantly. *A bad case of voodoo!*

Five

◇

"How's the cooking going with Todd?" Amy Sutton asked Elizabeth. It was Thursday afternoon and the two girls were sitting in a booth at Casey's, a popular ice cream parlor in the Valley Mall, sharing an enormous hot fudge sundae with extra whipped cream and cherries.

"Not so well, to be honest," Elizabeth said before putting a big spoonful of whipped cream in her mouth. "In fact, I wish I were just writing a book report for my social studies project instead. Anything that doesn't have to do with cooking."

"Why? What's the problem?" Amy asked.

"It's Todd. He's got the best intentions and everything, so I don't want to discourage him. But ever since he discovered how much he likes writing, he's all excited about trying new things. He's a terrible cook, though. A couple of nights ago my entire family was gagging because of the corn bread we made together." Elizabeth poured more hot fudge over the ice cream.

"How hard can it be to make corn bread?" Amy asked.

"Don't ask," Elizabeth said wearily. "I don't know how we're going to manage to make an entire meal for the social studies class."

"I'm sure with a little more practice it will work out," Amy said.

"I hope you're right. What are you doing for your project, by the way?" Elizabeth asked.

"I'm actually really excited about it. I've been reading diaries of slaves and I'm reworking them into a play. I'm going to have different people act it out in front of the class."

"That sounds great," Elizabeth said. "I'd much rather be doing that."

Just then Todd walked into Casey's. She almost hoped he wouldn't see her, but he did. He waved and came over and sat down at their booth. Normally Elizabeth would have been happy to see Todd, but not today. "Hey, Todd." She managed a cheerful smile.

"Hi," Todd said excitedly. "I was hoping to find you here. I thought we could go back over to my house and try out some new recipes."

Oh, great. That's the last thing I feel like doing, Elizabeth thought grimly. She had purposely gone to Casey's to avoid another cooking session. She glanced at Amy, who gave her a look of sympathy.

"You know, I've been enjoying this whole cooking experience so much that I've decided to maybe become a chef someday," Todd said enthusiastically. "Maybe I'll go to one of those fancy cooking schools in France."

"That's a terrific idea," Amy said.

Elizabeth detected a slight giggle from Amy, so she kicked her under the table.

"Why don't I meet you at your house in a half hour?" Elizabeth said quickly. She wanted Todd to leave because she wasn't sure she or Amy would be able to hold back their giggles.

"Great. I'll see you there, Julia," Todd said with a smile.

"Julia?" Amy demanded as soon as he was out of earshot.

"Don't ask."

"Come on, Elizabeth. Tell me!" Amy said.

Elizabeth felt her cheeks turn pink, and she stared down at the table. "He calls me Julia Child. That's his cooking name for me. If you ever tell anyone that, I'll kill you."

Elizabeth tried to give Amy a threatening look and they both burst into laughter.

"What's so funny?" Jessica asked as she walked into Casey's and plopped down at Elizabeth and Amy's booth.

"Oh, nothing," Elizabeth said between giggles.

"Todd was just telling us that he wanted to

become a chef," Amy blurted out.

Jessica joined in the laughter. "After sampling that corn bread the other night, I think Todd should keep his options open. He's really a pathetic cook."

Elizabeth immediately stopped laughing. Even though Elizabeth had to agree with Jessica, it bothered her that her sister was making fun of Todd. "I don't know," she said defensively. "Maybe if he practices a little more he'll turn out to be a good chef after all. He's certainly trying hard enough."

"What are you doing for your social studies project?" Amy asked Jessica, realizing this was a good time to change the subject.

"Well, I can't say too much about it. It's a secret. But I'll tell you that it has to do with voodoo practices," Jessica said mysteriously.

Oh, no, Elizabeth thought. *I had no idea she was doing this voodoo stuff for class.*

"Sounds interesting," Amy said.

You'd better believe it's interesting, Elizabeth thought. *Interesting and silly.*

"Look, I have a major dilemma," Jessica said. "I have to have the best Scarlett O'Hara costume for Lila's party and I don't have anything to wear. I was just at Valley Fashions, but they didn't have one single thing that was even remotely right."

"Do what Scarlett did when she was going to meet Rhett Butler in jail and she didn't have anything to wear," Amy said excitedly. "Remember? All her dresses had been destroyed—"

"And she used the green velvet curtains to make a dress!" Jessica shrieked. "Thank you, Amy. That's a great suggestion. You're brilliant." Jessica grabbed a spoon and took the last bite of their sundae.

"Hey, no fair. That was my bite," Elizabeth said, annoyed. Jessica was forever taking bites off other people's plates. Especially hers.

"Oh, sorry," Jessica said. "I guess I just got so excited. The curtains in our living room will be perfect."

Elizabeth was imagining the look on her mother's face if she came home and found Jessica wearing the living room curtains. "Jess, maybe that's not such a great idea. I mean, Mom would probably have a conniption if you used her curtains," Elizabeth cautioned. But she already knew it was too late to change her twin's mind. Jessica had that determined, excited look in her eye that Elizabeth knew too well.

"Don't worry. Mom and Dad are going out Friday night. I'll just wear them for the party and put them back before they come home," Jessica said. "And Lizzie," she continued in her sweetest voice, "I'm going to have to ask you a teeny-weeny favor."

Elizabeth was afraid she knew what was coming. No matter how hard she tried, she was never able to refuse her sister a favor.

"I need you to help me with the curtains," Jessica said.

"But you know I don't know how to sew," Elizabeth said.

"We don't really have to do any sewing. We'll just do a little pinning up here and there. That's all. There's no way I could manage all by myself. Please, please, please," Jessica said.

"Oh, I don't know," Elizabeth said with a sigh. "Buy me another hot fudge sundae with extra whipped cream and cherries and I'll think about it."

"Now add one half teaspoon of Tabasco." It was later that afternoon and Elizabeth was reading to Todd from the fish gumbo recipe. The Wilkins' kitchen was a total disaster area. There were fish bones and chopped-up vegetables all over the floor and counters, and dirty containers and utensils spilling over in the sink.

"I'm sorry, did you say five teaspoons of Tabasco?" Todd asked.

Just stay cool, Elizabeth said to herself silently. She was really on the edge of losing her temper. *How can Todd be such a good student at school and such a bumbler in the kitchen? How will I ever get through this without going out of my mind?*

"No, that's *one half* teaspoon of Tabasco," Elizabeth repeated slowly.

"Oh, oops!" Todd said giggling. "I already put in five teaspoons. I'll just put in more of whatever the next ingredient is to even it out a little bit."

"You put in five teaspoons already?" Elizabeth gasped.

"Yeah, so? I like to be a little creative when I

cook. Anyway, I don't think it's a good idea to stick too closely to the recipe," Todd said.

"You don't?" Elizabeth asked.

"No. Most of the best chefs of the world don't even follow recipes. They just go with the moment and the feeling. They're really more like artists than most people realize," Todd said as he stirred the gumbo with exaggerated, sweeping motions.

"I didn't know that," Elizabeth mumbled skeptically.

"OK, what's next?" Todd asked.

"Three cups of chopped celery," Elizabeth said even more slowly.

"So, we'll make that six cups of celery to make up for the extra Tabasco," Todd said.

If this relationship endures this cooking project, I'll know it's true love, Elizabeth thought as Todd piled on the celery and the soup slopped over onto the floor.

"Nice shot," Joe Howell was saying to Steven in the Wakefields' driveway after school on Thursday. Joe was Steven's best friend and Janet Howell's brother. The two boys were both ninth graders and members of the Sweet Valley High junior varsity basketball team.

"Hi, Joe," Jessica said as she passed the boys on her way into the house. Suddenly she had a great idea. Jessica knew how seriously Steven took basketball and how competitive he was with

Joe—especially over girls and basketball. Jessica couldn't pass up the opportunity to cause trouble.

She ran upstairs and grabbed her Steven doll and a pencil. She leaned out her window so she had a good view of them. "Double, double toil and trouble; Fire burn and cauldron bubble. Let my voodoo take a chance, and send my brother into a dance."

Jessica proceeded to poke the Steven doll over and over again with the eraser end of the pencil. To her amazement, the real Steven went into a spasmodic dance around the driveway and fumbled the ball.

This is amazing! Jessica thought. *I have total power over him.*

She was almost in a daze as she lay down on her bed and started daydreaming. Once people found out about her powers, she would be a celebrity! She imagined herself on the cover of all the major magazines and being asked to donate her services to the government to help deal with foreign enemies. She was sure that the Sweet Valley Police Department would be begging for her help. If they were trying to catch a criminal, she would just break a leg of a voodoo doll, and the criminal would be unable to run away.

Jessica took the Benjamin doll out of the shoe box and brought it downstairs with her to the kitchen. She reheated the healing potion on the stove then took the bowl back upstairs to her room.

She spread the potion over the doll's right leg. "Double, double toil and trouble; Fire burn and cauldron bubble. Take away this boy's pain, so he'll never need a cane."

If this works, she thought, *I'll donate my abilities to the medical community. I'll probably be flown all over the world to help cure people with rare diseases. My family and friends will be so proud of me.*

Jessica ran back downstairs and sat on the steps outside to watch Steven and Joe play basketball. She heard them laughing uncontrollably as she opened the back door.

The laughing stopped as soon as they saw Jessica.

"What's so funny?" Jessica asked.

"Your brother just told a really funny joke," Joe said. He was obviously trying not to laugh.

"I'm going to go get us some sodas," Steven said.

Joe looked at her with a serious expression as soon as Steven had gone inside the house. "You know, your brother's been acting really weird lately."

"How do you mean?" Jessica asked.

"Well, it's hard to describe. It's almost as if he's been walking around like a zombie or something. Today in math class he just sat there silently as our teacher was calling on him. It was weird. It was like he didn't hear what the teacher was saying," Joe said as he twirled the basketball around on the tip of his finger.

"Hmmmmm. Interesting," Jessica said as if she were a scientist conducting an experiment. "Anything else unusual that you've noticed lately?"

"As a matter of fact, just a few minutes ago he started dancing around, making strange noises, while we were in the middle of a game. It was bizarre," he said.

Jessica couldn't keep herself from smiling. She was really turning Steven into a walking zombie. *Now you'll think twice before you destroy my things, Steven Wakefield*, she thought triumphantly.

Six

◇

Jessica leapt out of bed when she remembered it was Friday morning. Lila's party was that night and she couldn't wait. She also knew that tonight Steven had a big date with Cathy Connors. She took out the Steven doll and grabbed a red Magic Marker from her desk.

"This should ruin your plans for romance," she said as she drew an enormous pimple on Steven's left cheek.

As she walked by the bathroom in the hallway she heard a loud shriek. Steven ran through the door, covering his face.

"What's wrong with you?" Jessica asked.

"None of your business," Steven barked.

At breakfast, Jessica couldn't believe her eyes. Steven had a big festering pimple on his left cheek.

"I've got some cover-up you can put on that thing," Jessica offered sweetly.

Steven just glared at Jessica and said nothing.

"Did you just get that pimple this morning?" Jessica asked.

"As a matter of fact, Dr. Wakefield, it's been growing all week. Now, mind your own business," Steven said, grabbing the platter of pancakes.

I don't remember seeing it this week, Jessica thought to herself.

"Jessica, honey, what did you decide to wear as your Scarlett dress tonight?" Mrs. Wakefield asked.

Jessica looked across the table at Elizabeth with an expression that said, *Keep your mouth shut.*

"Actually, I'm borrowing something," Jessica mumbled quickly.

"Do you think we could open the *curtains* in here?" Elizabeth said, smiling at Jessica. Elizabeth couldn't resist the opportunity to tease Jessica a little bit.

Jessica felt as if she were about to burst. "I'd prefer to keep them *closed*," she said, glaring at her sister.

"What are you dressing up as tonight, Elizabeth?" Mr. Wakefield asked.

"I was planning on going as Sojourner Truth, but I'm not sure I'll be able to go at all. I'm afraid Todd and I are going to have to practice our cooking tonight," Elizabeth said wearily.

"Who's Sojourner Truth?" Jessica asked.

"Jess, we just learned about her in our social

studies class. You were sitting right next to me," Elizabeth said.

"That's a big surprise," Steven said sarcastically. "If it didn't have to do with Johnny Buck or clothes, I'm sure it went right over Jessica's head."

Jessica was getting better at ignoring Steven's rude comments ever since she started her voodoo. Luckily, she had the Steven doll in her lap, and she gave it a couple of pokes on its left arm with her fork.

"Ouch," Steven exclaimed as he grabbed his left arm.

"What's wrong?" Mrs. Wakefield asked.

"I just had a little pain. I've been having a lot of strange little aches and pains lately. I don't know what's going on," Steven said shaking his head.

"So who is Sojourner Truth, anyway?" Jessica asked.

"She was a runaway slave, like Harriet Tub-man," Elizabeth said.

"Oh, right. Now I remember," Jessica lied.

"Hey, Jessica, are you going to Lila's party tonight?" Aaron Dallas asked as he walked up to Jessica's locker that morning after social studies class.

Aaron Dallas was one of the best-looking guys at Sweet Valley Middle School, and he was also Jessica's sort-of boyfriend. Normally Jessica spent a lot of her time thinking about boys, especially

Aaron. Even *she* would admit that she was boy-crazy. Lately, though, she'd been so preoccupied with her voodoo that she hadn't thought about boys much at all.

As she looked at Aaron now, with his wavy dark-blond hair and gorgeous smile, she remembered how much she really liked him. She wanted to be as pretty as ever tonight at the party.

"I wouldn't miss it for the world," Jessica said, flipping her hair to the side.

"Yeah, I think it should be pretty cool," Aaron said. "I kind of think the costume part is dumb, though."

"Aren't you going to dress up as anything?" Jessica asked.

"I figured I'd go as Rhett Butler," he said. "I guess that's what most of the guys are going as. What about you?"

"I'm dressing up as Scarlett, of course," Jessica said.

Just then, Lila came bounding over to Jessica's locker. "Aaron," she said, batting her eyelashes at him, "do you know what the best Rhett Butler gets as a prize tonight?" Lila asked flirtatiously.

"No. What?" Aaron asked.

"The first dance with me," Lila gushed.

"Then I'll just have to make sure I'm the best Rhett Butler," Aaron said, smiling at Lila. "I hate to lose at anything."

Lila is making me sick, Jessica thought. *She knows I*

like Aaron. She's just getting back at me for teasing her about the square dancing.

"I have an idea," Jessica said as Janet and Bruce Patman gathered around Jessica's locker. "I think it makes more sense for the best Rhett to have the first dance with the best Scarlett. What do you think, Janet?"

Jessica was so grateful that Janet walked up when she did. She knew that Lila would be forced to go along with whatever Janet said.

"That's a great idea," Janet said enthusiastically. "Since I'm judging the Scarletts, I guess it makes sense for me to judge the Rhetts, too."

"Oh, OK. I guess you're right," Lila said dejectedly.

"Are you planning on wearing a costume, Bruce?" Jessica asked.

"I wasn't planning on dressing up as anything at first, because I thought the whole idea was pretty babyish," Bruce said. "But I can't resist a contest, so I guess I'll probably dress like Rhett Butler. He seemed like a pretty cool dude, after all."

Jessica wasn't sure if she wanted Bruce or Aaron to win the contest. Even though she thought Bruce was a bore, she would love the chance to dance with him at the party. It would make a great impression on the other Unicorns, since he was the most popular guy in school.

Once the guys left, Jessica, Janet, and Lila walked down the hall and ran into Ellen and Tamara. The five girls headed outside together and plopped down on the grass under a big tree.

"I was thinking it would be fun for us to get ready at your house tonight, Jessica," Ellen said.

"What time should we come over?" Tamara asked.

It was sort of a Unicorn ritual to get ready for parties at Jessica's house. But tonight that ritual would have to be changed. Jessica didn't want them there while she was putting her curtain dress together.

"You know, maybe it's a better idea if we all get ready separately. Since most of us are competing for the Best Scarlett prize, it makes sense to wait until the last minute to show our costumes to one another," Jessica said.

"I think Jessica has a good point," Janet said.

Thanks, Janet. You've been saying all the right things so far, Jessica thought happily. She crossed her fingers. *Let's just hope you say the right thing tonight.*

On her way home from school, Jessica walked by Sweet Valley High and saw Steven standing on the lawn talking with Cathy Connors. He was obviously flirting with her and telling his usual dumb jokes.

Jessica stopped behind a tree where she was pretty sure she couldn't be seen. She took the Steven doll out from her backpack and turned the doll upside down. For a minute, she thought she saw Steven looking over in her direction, but he didn't give any sign that he'd seen her. *I must just be getting paranoid*, Jessica thought.

The next thing she knew, the real Steven was bending over and standing on his hands. He really looked ridiculous doing that in front of Cathy.

Jessica heard peals of laughter coming from Cathy.

"What has come over you, Steven Wakefield?" Cathy asked. "I hope you're not planning on acting like this tonight at the movies."

"Oh, it's nothing to worry about," Steven said when he stood back up on his two feet. "Just a little . . . uh, spell."

Spell? Did he just say what I thought he said? Jessica wondered nervously.

"You know, a dizzy spell," Steven continued. "Sometimes doing a handstand makes me feel better." Suddenly he looked up. "Hey, Jessica, is that you?" he yelled over toward the tree.

Jessica quickly stuffed the doll back into her bag and stood still.

"Boo!" Steven shouted as he jumped right in front of Jessica. "What are you doing there? Spying on me?"

"Uh . . . um . . . well . . ." Jessica could not think of one thing to say.

"Hi there, Jessica," Cathy said. "What's up?"

"Oh, hi, Cathy. I was just on my way home from school and I thought Steven might like to walk home with me," Jessica said, trying to make her voice sound normal.

"That's a great idea," Steven said cheerfully.

Boy, he really is acting weird, Jessica thought.

"I'll pick you up at seven-thirty tonight, OK?" Steven yelled to Cathy as he walked away.

"That's great," Cathy yelled back.

"Let me carry your backpack for you," Steven said to Jessica.

Before Jessica could say anything, Steven grabbed her backpack and flung it over his shoulder.

"What do you have in here? A brick?" Steven asked.

"Oh, just a lot of books," Jessica said quickly.

They walked awhile in silence. "I'm really glad we have this chance to spend a little time together," Steven said finally.

"You are?" Jessica asked in disbelief.

"Yeah, I am. Don't look so surprised. This walking home together was your idea, don't forget," Steven said. It seemed to Jessica that he was stifling a laugh.

"You're right," Jessica said.

"So, what's on your mind?" Steven asked.

"What do you mean?"

"Well, you must have something you wanted to talk to me about, right? Why else did you want to walk home together?"

"Oh. Right. Well, I just wanted to . . . uh . . . let you know that Mom and Dad will be out tonight and I'll be going to Lila's party, so you'll have to take care of your own dinner." Jessica herself couldn't believe what a lame excuse that was.

"That's it?" Steven asked.

"Yes, that's it," Jessica insisted.

"Are you sure?" Steven probed.

"Yes, I'm sure." Jessica was so relieved when they finally arrived at their house. She grabbed her backpack from Steven and quickly ran toward the house.

"That was great, walking home with you!" Steven yelled out to her as she walked into the house.

Seven

"I hope this temporary-perm kit works," Jessica said nervously to Elizabeth.

The twins were in the bathroom that connected their bedrooms. Elizabeth was keeping Jessica company while she fixed her hair for the party. Jessica's hair was covered up by a towel, and the room was a complete mess. There were curlers and bobby pins scattered all over the place.

"I'm having a hard time breathing in here. That smell is terrible," Elizabeth said, holding her nose. "Are you sure all those chemicals from that permanent kit aren't bad for your hair?"

"Who cares? All I care about is having perfect, curly locks like Scarlett," Jessica said.

"Don't you think Mom will get mad about you

giving yourself a permanent without asking her first?" Elizabeth asked.

"It's only temporary. It comes out after one or two shampoos," Jessica said.

"Didn't the Scarlett in the movie have brown hair?" Elizabeth asked as she read the ingredients on the permanent box.

"Yes, she did. That's why I washed my hair with this before I gave myself the permanent," Jessica said as she handed an empty shampoo bottle to Elizabeth.

"Hair dye?" Elizabeth said in disbelief. "Jess, what did you do to yourself?"

"I'm determined to be the spitting image of Scarlett O'Hara tonight. I want everything to be perfect."

"Don't you think dyeing your hair is a little extreme?" Elizabeth asked.

"No, I don't," Jessica said defensively. "It's not really a dye. It's just a rinse. Besides, I always wondered what I'd look like as a brunette."

"Well, what if the rinse doesn't come out?"

"It will. It says on the box that it's temporary."

"But how do you know it really will?" Elizabeth demanded.

"Let's just say it doesn't come out, which it will, but let's just say it won't—so what? What's so terrible about having brown hair? How do we know blondes really have more fun?" Jessica said flippantly.

Elizabeth knew that Jessica must be sure the dye

would come out. She knew very well that Jessica adored being blond.

I hope you're right, Jess. Otherwise you're going to be sorry, Elizabeth worried silently.

"Don't you need to start getting ready yourself?" Jessica asked as she spread a green clay mask on her face.

"I don't know if I'm going to go at all," Elizabeth said, sighing deeply. "Todd and I were planning on cooking tonight. I'd go over after we finish, but I'm afraid it could take all night."

Elizabeth felt depressed. She loved the idea of going to the party at Lila's house and seeing everyone dressed up. She didn't like Lila very much, but she had to admit she threw incredible parties.

"Lizzie, you have to come," Jessica insisted. "I think this project has gotten a little too intense. I mean, all you do lately is cook. How boring."

"I know. You're right," Elizabeth agreed. "I wish we weren't doing this cooking thing at all, to be perfectly honest. Todd takes it so seriously that all the fun has gone out of it."

"Well, what if you just do the cooking yourself and leave Todd out of it?" Jessica suggested. "He'd probably be relieved."

"He would be devastated. He thinks he's doing a great job. He's really getting into it, Jess." Elizabeth shook her head. "It would really crush him if I cut him out of it at the last minute."

"I have an idea," Jessica said as her face lit up.

Oh, no, Elizabeth thought. *Here comes another Jessica Wakefield scheme.*

"What if you fix it so that there's no way Todd could make a mistake?" Jessica said with an excited gleam in her eye. Coming up with schemes was the thing she enjoyed most in the world.

"How do you mean?" Elizabeth asked skeptically.

Jessica thought for a moment. "What night will you actually cook the final meal?"

"The class is supposed to eat it next Wednesday, so Tuesday night we'll cook everything."

"OK, so here's what you do," Jessica began. "Before Todd comes over to cook on Tuesday, change all the ingredients around. And change the markings on the measuring cups. Just try to think ahead of what kind of mistakes he usually makes. Then he won't be able to mess it up," she finished, obviously pleased with herself.

It sounds pretty risky, but it might work, Elizabeth thought. She drummed her fingers on the counter. "You know, I might actually take your suggestion," she said.

"Great! So maybe you'll come to the party after all," Jessica said.

"Maybe we will. It seems like this really might work," Elizabeth said with a new enthusiasm. "I'm going to go look over the recipes and see if I can figure out a way to put your plan into action."

Elizabeth was sitting on Jessica's bed, looking at

a recipe book, when she heard a loud shriek from the bathroom. Jessica flung open the door and ran into her room in tears.

"I'm ruined! I'm ruined!" Jessica cried. She stood in front of her full-length mirror gaping in horror. Her hair was bright orange!

"Oh, no!" Elizabeth exclaimed. "What happened?"

Jessica could barely speak, she was so upset.

"Don't panic," Elizabeth said, trying to sound calm. "Let's just go shampoo it out. It will probably come right out."

"But then my perm will be ruined," Jessica said as the tears ran down her face. "All my plans for being the best Scarlett just went down the drain."

Elizabeth hated to see her twin upset. "OK, Jess, calm down. You have two choices," she said in her most rational voice. "You can go to the party with curly, orange hair or you can go with blond hair that just won't be quite as curly. We can still curl it a little bit with a curling iron."

Jessica went back into the bathroom to shampoo her hair while Elizabeth waited in Jessica's room, crossing her fingers.

Please come out. Please come out, Elizabeth pleaded silently.

At the same moment, Steven walked into Jessica's room from the hallway wearing his bathing suit and Jessica walked in from the bathroom. Jessica took the towel off her hair and stood in front of the mirror.

"Oh, my gosh!" Steven yelled. He was laughing so hard, he fell on the ground. "I didn't realize this was a Halloween party," he said between guffaws. "I see you dressed up as the Great Pumpkin. Is this a new fashion look they're showing in the magazines these days? I guess you're just on the cutting edge."

Jessica burst into tears as she looked in the mirror. "Get out of here, Steven Wakefield!" she yelled. "You're a horrible, awful brother and I'll make you regret you ever stepped into this room!"

"See ya, Carrot Top," Steven said as he left the room in hysterical laughter. "I'll be taking a swim if you need some fashion tips." Jessica plopped face down on her bed and cried.

"There's no way I can go to the party now. I'll be the laughingstock of Sweet Valley," Jessica sobbed.

"Wait, I have an idea," Elizabeth said. "Stay right here. I'll be back in a minute. Don't worry."

Jessica looked out the window at Steven splashing around in the pool and was overcome with rage. *You're really going to get it now,* she thought to herself as she picked up the Steven doll. She took the doll downstairs and stood on the deck by the pool where Steven was standing on the diving board. Just as Steven was about to take a dive, she twirled the doll around backwards. Steven let out a yell and nearly banged his head on the diving board as he did a belly flop into the water.

For a minute, Jessica's heart stopped as she looked into the pool and waited for Steven to resurface. She saw him floating face down in the water, then finally get up for air.

"Uh . . . Steven? Are you OK?" She stepped out into the light of the deck.

"Yeah, sure." He looked at her and laughed. "I'm fine. It's you I'm worried about, Carrot Top."

Jessica ran back into the house and up the stairs to her room. *You better not tease me, you jerk,* Jessica thought angrily. *I have total power over you.*

She looked in the mirror and saw her bright-orange hair. A little chill went up her spine. *I really look like a witch now. Maybe I'm being punished for my voodoo.*

At this rate she'd never get a prize at the party. Not unless they gave out a prize for best witch.

"Listen, Jess, get a hold of yourself," Elizabeth was saying as she came back into Jessica's room. She was carrying the living room curtains, scissors, a big roll of gold rope, and a wide-brimmed straw hat. "You're going to go to Lila's party and you're going to win the Best Scarlett prize."

"But how can I possibly go with my hair like this?" Jessica moaned, lying back on her bed.

"Remember in the movie when Scarlett wears the curtains to visit Rhett? She wears a big hat," Elizabeth said excitedly.

Jessica sat up in her bed and wiped a stray tear away. "So?"

"So you're going to wear this hat and nobody will be able to see your hair at all," Elizabeth said.

"Where did you find that?" Jessica asked.

"It's Mom's gardening hat," Elizabeth said.

"I'll be laughed out of the party if I wear that thing," Jessica said.

"It's all a question of attitude," Elizabeth argued. "If you walk into that party feeling like the most beautiful Scarlett, then you'll win the contest hands down."

"Do you really think it will work?" Jessica asked sheepishly.

"Have I ever let you down?" Elizabeth asked.

"Never, ever, ever," Jessica said. She leaned over on the bed and gave her sister a big hug. "You're the best sister in the world."

"Let's fix your dress first. Get off of that bed," Elizabeth commanded.

Jessica stood up in front of the mirror while Elizabeth wrapped the curtains around her. She wrapped the rope around Jessica in a way that made her waist look extra tiny. The curtains fell down to the ground and made a super full skirt. Elizabeth gathered the curtains around Jessica's arms with safety pins, which made a great, old-fashioned-sleeve effect.

"This looks great!" Jessica exclaimed. "I can't believe how talented you are. It doesn't even look like curtains!"

Elizabeth looked up and down at Jessica,

pleased with her handiwork. "Now we have to take care of the hair situation."

Elizabeth plopped the big straw hat on Jessica's head and tucked all the hair in it. She tied a big purple bow around the crown to finish off the look.

"Ta-da!" Elizabeth said triumphantly.

Jessica glanced in the mirror. Not one single strand of orange hair could be seen.

"You really think no one will know what's under this hat?" Jessica asked hopefully.

"No way," Elizabeth said, sounding more confident than she felt. "Just make sure of one thing," she warned.

"What's that?"

"If you dance, make sure you don't move around too quickly or your hat will fall off."

"Good suggestion," Jessica said.

"Why don't you practice?"

"That's a good idea," Jessica said. "I think there's going to be square dancing tonight, so why don't you pretend to be Aaron and twirl me around?"

"OK," Elizabeth said, grabbing Jessica's hand and spinning her around the room. "Do-si-do your partner, allemande right and bring her on home. Twirl that girl around the room," Elizabeth said in her best square-dance-caller imitation.

The two girls broke into giggles and collapsed on her bed.

"Is my hat still in place?" Jessica asked fearfully, after her giggles subsided.

"Absolutely perfect," Elizabeth said.

"By the way, how do you know those square-dancing calls?" Jessica asked.

"I love square dancing," Elizabeth said as she straightened out Jessica's costume. "That was my favorite part of music class when we were in the fourth grade."

Jessica shook her head. "Sometimes I really can't believe we're sisters," she teased.

"You better watch it or I'll pull that hat off in the middle of the party," Elizabeth teased back.

"OK, OK. Truce," Jessica said.

Eight

◇

"I'll never be hungry again!" Jessica said.

"I'll think about that tomorrow," Lila said.

"Fiddle-dee-dee!" Tamara said.

Most of the girls were walking around Lila's beautiful house and gardens, quoting Scarlett O'Hara lines from *Gone With the Wind*. Every Scarlett thought she was the best one.

When Jessica first saw Lila's elaborate, expensive dress, she almost ran out the front door in tears. Lila's dress was covered with detailed, gold-embroidered drawings. It had a teeny waist and a full skirt. Lila's hair had been curled and looked exactly like Scarlett's in the movie. Even Lila's accent seemed to be perfect. *It's just not fair*, Jessica thought. *Lila always gets the best things because she's so rich. I'm sure she's going to win.*

Jessica was standing at the refreshment table, feeling sorry for herself, when Aaron Dallas, Patrick Morris, and Denny Jacobson came up to her. All three boys were dressed like Rhett Butler.

"Hey, Jessica, you really look terrific," Aaron gushed.

"Yeah, that's a super costume," Denny said. Denny was one of the cutest guys in the eighth grade, and Jessica had a bit of a crush on him.

"Thanks!" There was nothing Jessica loved more than getting attention from boys. Especially cute ones. Suddenly her mood totally changed and she felt pretty and popular again. She remembered what Elizabeth had said about attitude.

"You guys look pretty great yourselves," Jessica said as she batted her eyelashes in Scarlett fashion.

"Where'd you get your dress, Jessica?" Caroline Pearce, the biggest gossip at Sweet Valley Middle School, asked, appearing at Jessica's elbow. "The linen department at the Valley Mall? What are those anyway? Curtains?"

"I think Jessica has the prettiest dress at the party," Aaron said, coming to her rescue.

"Who are you supposed to be?" Jessica asked Caroline.

"Scarlett, of course," Caroline said before she walked off in a huff.

"Thanks for sticking up for me," Jessica said.

"I wouldn't pay any attention to her. She's just jealous," Patrick said.

"Hey, Lila, your place looks great," Aaron said as Lila joined their group by the refreshment table.

"Thanks," Lila gushed. "I'm pretty pleased by the way it turned out."

The place really did look spectacular. The tall trees were strewn with twinkling white lights. There were flowers hanging from every imaginable place, and the tables were overflowing with every kind of Southern cuisine. The house and lawn really did look like the grand mansions in *Gone With the Wind*.

"Jessica, dahling," Ellen said in a bad Southern accent. "How are ya'll doin'?"

"That's a great dress, Ellen," Jessica said in her sincerest-sounding voice. She knew Ellen would expect her to be jealous of her dress and she didn't want to give her that satisfaction.

Janet joined the group, wearing an equally stunning, yet plainer dress. She was dressed up as Melanie.

"You know, in the movie, Scarlett was trying to take my husband, Ashley, away," Janet said. "I'd really be in trouble tonight if this were the real thing, considering how many Scarletts are walking around here."

"Is it true that this party is going to be your social studies project for The Hairnet's class?" Aaron asked.

"Absolutely," Lila bragged. "I even hired a photographer to take pictures of everything to show in class when I make my presentation. I have a feeling mine will be the best project in the class."

"I wouldn't be too sure about that," Jessica said in front of the large group that was formed around the refreshment table.

"Oh, really?" Patrick Morris asked. "What are you doing for your project?"

"Well, I don't want to spoil the surprise." Jessica's eyes were widening under her big, straw hat as she felt all the attention on her. "I will only say that it's probably going to scare a lot of people. In fact, I don't think any of you will have seen anything like it before in your lifetime."

"Sounds interesting," Denny said. "Maybe I'll stop in."

"I'll be there," Bruce Patman said. "I'd like to know what's so scary."

"The entire school should come to class that day," Jessica said. "I can guarantee that it will be an event no one will want to miss."

"Hey, Jess! How's the party?" Elizabeth asked breathlessly.

Jessica was walking into the house from the backyard when the twins practically ran into each other.

"You finally made it. I was starting to worry about you," Jessica said.

"I can't wait to get on the square-dancing floor," Elizabeth said.

"You can't dance now," Jessica said frantically.

"Why not?"

"Because the contest winners are about to be an-

nounced and I need you to come to the bathroom
with me to make sure my costume's perfect,"
Jessica pleaded.

Elizabeth dutifully followed Jessica into the ex-
pansive bathroom off the main hallway.

"Now, are you absolutely positive that you can't
see any orange hair?" Jessica asked.

"I promise. You know I would tell you."

Elizabeth smoothed out Jessica's dress and
straightened her hat.

"Now, go out there and win that prize," Elizabeth commanded.

Just as Jessica and Elizabeth emerged from the
house, everyone started running toward them
shouting, "Congratulations!"

"What's going on?" Jessica asked.

"You missed the announcement," Amy cried.
"Janet said you're the best Scarlett O'Hara."

"All right!" Elizabeth shouted. She gave her sister a high five.

Jessica was beaming. Everyone was crowded
around her.

"Come on, Miss Scarlett," Aaron Dallas said, swag-
gering up to Jessica. "I believe it's time for our dance."

"Do you really want to square-dance?" Jessica
asked, scrunching up her face. That wasn't exactly
how she wanted to spend her moment of glory.

"Yes, indeed I do, Miss Scarlett," Aaron beamed.
"I love square dancing!"

"You do?" Jessica asked in disbelief.

"You bet!" Aaron answered.

Jessica couldn't put her finger on it, but there was something about Aaron that was starting to bug her. Maybe he was just a little too gushy about her. *He certainly doesn't seem much like the Rhett Butler in the movie,* Jessica thought to herself.

As soon as Jessica's dance with Aaron ended, Patrick Morris tapped Aaron on the shoulder and cut in. When their dance ended, Denny Jacobson tapped Patrick on the shoulder. One after the other, different guys kept coming up to Jessica to dance with her. Jessica was in absolute heaven. When Bruce Patman and she were dancing, she looked around to make sure all the Unicorns were watching. To her total joy, all eyes were on her.

I really am Scarlett O'Hara tonight! This is one of the best parties of my life. Jessica was even starting to like square dancing!

"Jessica!" Elizabeth said urgently, running up to her.

"What's wrong, Lizzie?" Jessica was standing by the pool, gossiping with a group of Unicorns.

"It's time to go," Elizabeth said, looking at her watch.

"But the party's still in full swing," Lila said. "Don't tell me you guys have a bedtime."

Don't tempt me or I'll push you in the pool, Lila Fowler, Jessica thought.

"The curtains," Elizabeth whispered to Jessica.

"We don't have a bedtime. We just . . . um . . ." Jessica was having one of those rare moments when she couldn't think of what to say.

"We don't want all the guys to have a big fight over Jessica, so we thought we should leave before things get out of control," Elizabeth said, saving the day.

I owe you big time for tonight, Lizzie, Jessica thought gratefully.

"Let's go," Elizabeth said, pulling her sister by the arm. "Amy's father is waiting in the car."

Minutes later, Jessica and Elizabeth jumped out of the Suttons' car and raced into their house. They ran up the stairs and into Jessica's room, where Elizabeth dismantled the curtains.

"Mom said they'd be home by ten o'clock. That's in five minutes," Elizabeth said, panicking.

"Wait a minute," Jessica said on their way down the stairs with the curtains. "What about my hair? I can't let Mom and Dad see me like this."

"Here," Elizabeth said as she threw a beret at Jessica. "Put that on. Fast!"

They sprinted down the stairs and frantically put the curtains back up over the windows.

They had just finished putting up the last panel when they heard their parents' car pulling into the driveway.

The twins jumped on the couch in the living room and flipped open magazines at the exact moment their parents walked in the door.

"How was the party?" Mrs. Wakefield asked.

"Oh, super," Jessica said calmly.

"Just great," Elizabeth agreed.

Nine

"Wake up! Wake up!" Jessica shouted at Elizabeth as she bounced on her bed on Saturday morning.

Elizabeth opened one eye, then buried her head under the pillow. Normally Jessica was the one who slept late. Elizabeth was always trying to get *her* out of bed.

"What are you doing up so early on a Saturday morning?" Elizabeth asked in a sleepy voice.

"I washed my hair five times and look at me!" Jessica said excitedly.

Elizabeth sat up slowly in bed and rubbed her eyes.

"Your hair! It's totally back to normal. That's great."

"Thank goodness. I think I would have had to move away from Sweet Valley until my blond hair grew back in if the rinse hadn't come out," Jessica said with a sigh of relief.

"I hope you're never going to dye your hair again," Elizabeth said.

"I never like to say never," Jessica teased.

"How was your date last night with Cathy?" Jessica asked Steven at the breakfast table that morning.

"I didn't end up going," Steven mumbled to himself.

"Why's that?" Jessica persisted.

"Not that it's any of your business, but I wasn't feeling very well," Steven said.

Jessica was hiding the Steven doll on her lap under the table, and when she thought nobody was watching, she spilled a little milk on its shirt. To Jessica's delight, Steven spilled milk on his shirt at almost exactly the same time!

Jessica couldn't resist trying it again, so she took a spoonful of honey and dripped it on the doll's chin.

"Stop eating like a pig," Elizabeth said to Steven as he wiped a big glob of honey from his chin.

This is truly amazing! Jessica thought. *I've got total power over him!*

"Steven, do you think you're coming down with something? You don't really seem like yourself," Mrs. Wakefield said in a concerned voice.

He's always a slob, Jessica thought to herself.

"No, I'm OK. Although I have had some strange experiences lately," Steven said.

"What kind of experiences?" Mr. Wakefield asked.

"Like little aches and pains and feeling spaced out. Also, I've had a hard time sleeping," Steven said, staring off into space.

"It's probably just your age. I remember going through periods like that myself when I was fourteen," Mr. Wakefield said.

"What kind of stuff did you do?" Elizabeth asked.

"Oh, let's see. . . . One time I was in my American history class and I was supposed to get up in front of the class and give an oral report about Patrick Henry," Mr. Wakefield said.

"Who is Patrick Henry?" Jessica asked.

"Good grief!" Steven said, rolling his eyes.

"He was one of the framers of the Constitution," Elizabeth said. "He's the one that said, 'Give me liberty or give me death.'"

"Oh, yeah, now I remember," Jessica lied.

"Yeah, right," Steven said sarcastically.

Watch it, Steven, Jessica thought to herself. *I could wring this doll like a washcloth if I wanted to.*

"Anyway, I was standing in front of the class," Mr. Wakefield continued, "and I couldn't for the life of me remember what I was doing. I had been daydreaming so much that I forgot everything. I had no idea who Patrick Henry was or why I was standing in front of the class."

"And so what happened?" Jessica asked eagerly.

"So the classroom was completely quiet except for a few giggles here and there. And—I started singing," Mr. Wakefield said.

"What do you mean? What did you sing?" Mrs. Wakefield asked, obviously amused.

" 'Yankee Doodle Dandy,' " Mr. Wakefield said.

All the Wakefields burst into laughter.

"So anyway," Mr. Wakefield said, trying to catch his breath, "the point is that sometimes daydreaming and spacing out are just normal parts of growing up."

That may be true, Jessica thought to herself, *but voodoo has a lot to do with it, too.*

"Jessica, I thought you should know that Bruce and Aaron were fighting over you after you left the party last night," Tamara said. She sighed. "You must be totally psyched."

It was Saturday afternoon and the Unicorns were doing what they enjoyed most—shopping at the mall. They were trying on hats, sunglasses, belts, and scarves in the accessory department at Kendall's.

"Yeah, they are two of the most popular guys at Sweet Valley Middle School," Ellen agreed as she flung a scarf around her neck.

"It was pretty great, I must admit," Jessica said, trying not to sound too excited.

"Where *did* you get that dress, Jessica? You never told us," Lila said suspiciously.

"It was pretty unusual," Janet said as she threw an enormous straw hat on her head. "I've never seen anything like it in the stores around here."

Jessica was trying on some oversized white plastic sunglasses and trying to change the subject. "What do you all think of the glasses?" she asked, striking a pose.

"Very sixties," Ellen said. "So, where *did* you get that dress, Jessica?"

What is this? The Spanish Inquisition? Why does everybody care so much about my dress? No matter what, Jessica was not going to give away her secret.

"Well, if you must know . . ." Jessica began. She paused while she thought of a good story. She knew she was good at making up stories on the spur of the moment. She didn't really consider it lying—just using her imagination in a positive way.

"My great-great-great-great-great-grandmother," Jessica started, "kept a big trunk of all her old dresses. She gave the trunk to her daughter, who gave it to her daughter, and on and on."

"So your grandmother gave it to your mother and she gave it to you," Lila said.

Jessica wasn't sure but she thought she saw Lila roll her eyes at Janet.

"Exactly," Jessica said matter-of-factly.

"I just have one more question," Ellen said. "What else is in that trunk?"

"Oh, there are lots of beautiful dresses and uniforms from the Civil War," Jessica gushed. Once she started with her stories, she had a hard time stopping.

"Wow, that sounds really cool," Ellen said.

"Maybe you should bring the uniforms in to show our social studies class. I'm sure Mrs. Arnette would love it."

"How about if we have a Unicorn meeting at your house and try on some of those old dresses?" Janet suggested.

"Great idea!" Lila said.

"Let's go over after we leave the mall," Ellen said.

"Um . . . actually, I don't think my mom would really like that very much." Jessica's mind was racing. "Most of the clothes are pretty brittle, since they're so old. She wasn't really thrilled about me wearing that dress to the party." She grabbed Lila's wrist and looked at her watch. "Whoops! I'm supposed to meet up with Elizabeth at the pizza place. See ya guys later!"

Phew! That was a close call, Jessica thought as she walked out of the store. *The secret of the winning dress will never be revealed!*

"Where's your cane?" Jessica asked Benjamin as she plopped herself down at the booth in the pizzeria where he was sitting with Elizabeth and Amy Sutton.

"I didn't need it today," Benjamin said. He was smiling as he finished off a big bite of pizza. "My leg has been a hundred times better lately."

"Wow! You're kidding! That's great!" Jessica said enthusiastically. "The pain is totally gone?" She shot a triumphant look at her sister.

"Not totally, but almost. I still have it a little bit when I wake up in the morning. But the best thing is that I don't have it at night anymore. I haven't been as tired lately because I'm sleeping well," Benjamin said.

I'm a medical genius! Jessica was thinking to herself. *I'll have to start doing my healing in the mornings now, too.*

"Why do you think the pain went away?" Amy asked.

"I don't know. Even the doctor isn't quite sure," Benjamin said.

Maybe the doctor doesn't know, but I sure do, Jessica thought happily as she grabbed a piece of pizza. She looked at the pizza in her hand and smiled guiltily at Elizabeth. "Whoops! Sorry, I guess I was just excited about Benjamin's leg."

"You do know why Benjamin's leg is better, don't you?" Jessica asked Elizabeth as they walked around the mall together. Benjamin and Amy had just left to walk home.

"No, I don't. Why? Do you think you do?" Elizabeth asked.

"Yes, I do, as a matter of fact," Jessica said as they walked into the record store. "I think it's definitely because of my healing doll."

"You're not serious, are you?" Elizabeth asked.

"Of course I'm serious. You heard what he said. Not even the doctor understands why it's better,"

Jessica said as she flipped through the Johnny Buck CDs.

"Jessica, I'm sure there's a logical explanation."

"Oh, really? And what would that be?"

"I don't know," Elizabeth said, frustrated. "Sometimes medical problems just go away on their own. Who knows? Maybe it was some new drug he started taking. I just don't think you should go overboard with this voodoo thing."

"Well, look what's happened with Steven," Jessica said.

"What's happened with Steven?" Elizabeth asked.

"Elizabeth! How can you not have noticed? He has totally responded to my voodoo," Jessica said as she walked toward the counter with a new Johnny Buck CD in her hand.

"He has been acting weird lately," Elizabeth conceded. She shrugged. "But you know Steven. He's always weird."

"How about an ice cream sundae?" Jessica asked Elizabeth as they walked past Casey's later that afternoon.

"Aren't you full from that pizza?" Elizabeth asked. "Do you really feel like eating ice cream?"

"I always feel like eating ice cream," Jessica said.

As soon as they walked in, Jessica noticed Steven sitting in a booth at the back with Cathy Connors.

"Look who's here," Jessica said to Elizabeth.

"This gives me the perfect opportunity to show you how my voodoo works," she added in a whisper.

The twins sat down at a table across from Steven and Cathy.

"Don't you two want to join us?" Cathy asked.

"No, that's OK. We thought you two might like to be alone," Jessica said.

"We'd be happy to have you sit with us," Steven said.

What's with Steven? Elizabeth thought. Normally he would hate for them to be sitting so close to him when he was on a date. Jessica ordered two hot fudge sundaes from the waiter.

"I'll never be able to eat this," Elizabeth said as soon as the waiter brought over the enormous sundaes.

"You have to eat it," Jessica whispered urgently. "Otherwise it will be too obvious that we're here for another reason."

"Why *are* we here?" Elizabeth asked, exasperated.

"To show you how my voodoo works," Jessica said. "Now, watch this."

Jessica took out the Steven doll from her backpack. She gathered up a big spoonful of whipped cream and dribbled it on the doll's chin, holding it up a little so Elizabeth could see.

"Jess, what are you doing?" Elizabeth hissed.

"Shhhh," Jessica whispered. "Just look at Steven."

Elizabeth looked over at Steven. Sure enough, his face was covered with whipped cream.

"Steven, you're a total slob," Cathy said between giggles.

Steven shook his head. "You know, lately I've been feeling like there's some kind of curse on me," Steven said loud enough for his sisters to hear.

"See what I mean?" Jessica hissed triumphantly.

"How do you know he wasn't looking over here?" Elizabeth asked.

"He wasn't. Trust me," Jessica said, and she took a big bite of her sundae.

This is really getting ridiculous, Elizabeth thought.

"Lizzie, I was thinking that maybe you should write an article for the *Sixers* about my powers. I even think eventually all the local papers and TV shows will probably want to do stories on me. Who knows? Maybe I'll even get national coverage."

Elizabeth tried to keep her expression serious. "Why don't we wait and see if these powers really exist?"

Before going to sleep that night, Jessica hid behind Steven's door with the voodoo doll and a pencil. "Double, double toil and trouble; Fire burn and cauldron bubble. Make my brother into a zombie." First she flipped the doll around in the air a few times, then poked it with her pencil and gave it a few tugs and pulls.

To Jessica's great delight, Steven started squirming all around on his bed. It was all she could do not to laugh out loud.

She was about to head back to her room when she noticed something strange. She'd stopped poking and spinning the doll, but the real Steven continued to twitch and squirm in his bed.

Boy, I must have given him a powerful dose that time, she thought, holding the doll perfectly still. Jessica stood there and watched in amazement as he kept flailing and moaning for another several minutes.

"Jessica, is that you?" Steven called out in a weak voice, just as she was turning to go back to her room. She stood still in her tracks and almost dropped the doll on the ground. She walked a little ways down the hallway, then turned around and walked back toward his room so Steven wouldn't know she'd been standing there all along.

"What is it?" she asked breathlessly, expecting the worst.

"I just wanted to say goodnight," Steven said sweetly.

"Is that all?" Jessica asked, her heart pounding.

"Yeah. Oh, and I just wanted you to know that you're a really wonderful sister."

Jessica's mouth fell open in astonishment. *Maybe I really have gone too far!*

Ten

At breakfast on Sunday morning, Steven was as pale as a ghost, and there were big dark circles under his eyes.

"I barely slept at all last night," Steven said sleepily. "I kept tossing and turning and I had terrible dreams."

"That's it! You're going to the doctor tomorrow and you're staying home from school," Mrs. Wakefield said.

"Oh, I'm sure it's nothing," Steven said. "Maybe it's just a phase, like Dad was saying."

"You do what your mother says. This is starting to sound a little more serious than that," Mr. Wakefield said.

"That's a beautiful blouse you're wearing today, Jessica," Steven said out of the blue.

Jessica looked down at the purple-and-blue flowered T-shirt she was wearing. She wore it all the time. She'd had it for years.

Steven never notices what I'm wearing, Jessica thought to herself. Jessica stared at him for the rest of breakfast and noticed that he just stared off into space the whole time, looking like a zombie. There was the tiniest pang of worry in the pit of her stomach. *Why does he have to be so nice to me when I'm being so terrible to him?*

After school on Monday, Jessica walked into the family room and saw Steven lying on the couch, watching TV.

"Oh, hi, Jessica. How was school today?" Steven asked.

How was school today? He's never asked me how school was in his entire life, Jessica thought.

"School was fine, thanks," Jessica mumbled.

"Do you want to watch this with me? It's really good," Steven said.

"What are you watching?" Jessica asked.

"It's a documentary about ballet," Steven said.

Documentary? Ballet? This is getting scary, Jessica thought.

"You're looking very lovely today, Jessica," Steven said.

Jessica was stunned. "Thanks," she finally muttered. "Did you stay home from school today?"

"Yeah, I was still feeling pretty sick. I went to the

doctor and he did some tests on me," Steven said.

"And what did he say was wrong with you?" Jessica asked, suddenly feeling nervous.

"They won't know for a couple of days," Steven said.

I wonder if voodoo could somehow show up on the tests, Jessica thought.

That night Jessica had a terrible time falling asleep. She kept tossing and turning and thinking about Steven. What had she done to him?

It seemed as though her powers were even greater than she imagined. The Steven doll was lying peacefully on her desk, but down the hall the real Steven was moaning in his bed. *Had she lost control of her voodoo?* What if Steven really was sick and it was all her fault?

She put her pillow over her ears, so she wouldn't hear the moaning, and finally she fell asleep.

Jessica was swimming in the ocean, laughing and splashing, when suddenly an enormous wave came crashing down on her. She fell to the bottom of the ocean floor. Every time she tried to stand up, she was knocked back down again. She was choking on the water and she couldn't breathe.

She saw Steven sitting on the beach. She tried to yell h-- ame, but no sound came out of her mouth. ...ly Steven was in the water, trying to pull her out. He carried her toward the shore, where it was shallow, and Jessica was able to stand up and catch her breath.

She stood on the sand and looked back out toward the water. Steven was waving and smiling at her. She waved back to him just as another huge wave broke over him and knocked him down. She waited for him to resurface but he never did.

Jessica tried to walk into the water to save him but she was paralyzed. Her feet were stuck in the sand and she couldn't walk. She tried yelling, but again no words came out of her mouth.

Suddenly she was at Steven's funeral, sitting with Elizabeth and their parents. They were all crying uncontrollably. Jessica tried to comfort them, but nobody would look at her or talk to her. It was as if she had become invisible. "Steven, I'm sorry!" she moaned. "I didn't mean it!"

Jessica eyes flew open and she sat straight up in bed. She was covered in sweat and her heart was pounding. She was shaking all over and her skin felt ice-cold.

She quickly turned on the light in her room and looked in the mirror. *It was just a nightmare,* she kept telling herself. *I didn't kill Steven. He's fine.*

She knew what she needed to do. She needed to stop the voodoo immediately. There was still time to fix everything. She'd just quit the voodoo and Steven would be back to his normal self in no time.

*   *   *

Jessica woke up on Tuesday morning still a little shaky from her dream. Her eyes fell on the Steven doll lying on her desk, and she had an idea. She wasn't just going to stop tormenting her brother, she was going to help make him better.

She put the Steven doll next to the radio and set the dial to an easy-listening station. A corny version of the song "Feelings" was playing. Oh, well, she figured, it was probably soothing. She took the pillow from her bed and settled the doll into it. Before she left her room, she chanted, "Double, double toil and trouble; Fire burn and cauldron bubble. Let my voodoo be undone, and give my parents back their son."

Jessica's heart almost stopped when she walked into the kitchen for breakfast and saw that Steven's chair was empty.

"Where's Steven?" Jessica asked, her eyes wide.

"Relax, Jess, he's having his breakfast in bed," Elizabeth said. "He's still not feeling well."

"Did you . . . see him today?" Jessica asked.

"Yes, I saw him in his room," Elizabeth said.

"I just took him his breakfast," Mr. Wakefield said.

"You seem so upset, honey. What's wrong?" Mrs. Wakefield asked.

"Oh, nothing," Jessica lied as she sat down at the table. "I guess I'm just worried about Steven's health."

"I think that's sweet that you're so concerned

about your brother's welfare," Mrs. Wakefield said. "What a good sister you are."

Jessica stared at her place mat. *If you only knew*, she thought miserably.

On her way to school that morning, Jessica confessed her fears to Elizabeth.

"I really think I'm hurting him with my voodoo," Jessica said.

"Don't be silly. He's probably just got the flu or something. I honestly wouldn't give this voodoo stuff too much credit," Elizabeth said.

"But my dream seemed so real. He was dead and it was all my fault. It was so scary," Jessica said as they walked up the school steps.

"You're always saying you'd like to kill Steven," Elizabeth teased.

"This isn't funny, Lizzie," Jessica said. She was on the verge of tears.

"I'm sorry, Jess. Please don't cry. I'm one-hundred-percent positive that Steven is not under a curse or about to die or anything. Pull yourself together and stop worrying, OK?"

"How can you be so positive?" Jessica asked.

"Just trust me," Elizabeth said.

Jessica thought about Steven all day at school. She practically failed a math quiz because she couldn't concentrate. And she'd even studied a little the night before. She'd thought she had a pretty good understanding of the material, but all the numbers and formulas just blurred together on the page. She jotted down random answers that had nothing to do with the questions.

At Booster practice that afternoon, Jessica kept dropping her baton and forgetting the cheers.

"Come on, Jessica. Concentrate!" Janet yelled. "We have to learn this one."

"Oh, sorry," Jessica mumbled. She kept thinking about how she was going to try to reverse her voodoo. She would have to read in her book about how to undo voodoo curses.

She was so absorbed in her thoughts that she didn't hear the discussion the Unicorns were having about an upcoming bake sale.

"So what about you, Jessica?" Janet asked.

"What about me?" Jessica asked.

"What are you making for the bake sale?" Lila asked.

"What bake sale?" Jessica asked.

Lila looked at Janet and rolled her eyes. "The bake sale we've been planning for two weeks now. The one we're having to raise money for new batons," Lila said.

"Oh, right. I guess I'll make voodoo," Jessica said without realizing what she was saying.

All the Unicorns started laughing hysterically.

"What's so funny?" Jessica asked.

"You just said you were making voodoo for the bake sale," Ellen said.

"I said that? I meant to say that I'll make brownies," Jessica said.

"Are you feeling OK?" Janet asked.

"Actually, I'm not feeling so great. I think I'll go home a little bit early today," Jessica said. She quickly gathered up her things and ran out of the gym.

She ran all the way home. She needed to make sure Steven was OK.

Eleven

When Jessica got home from school, Steven was lying on the couch in the family room. The TV wasn't on and he was humming a tune. His eyes were closed and he kept twitching and wincing like he was in pain.

Suddenly Jessica froze in the doorway. That tune! Steven was humming "Feelings"! Jessica felt her stomach drop. Voodoo was more powerful than she ever imagined!

Jessica ran right up to her room and turned off the radio. She paced for a while before she took out the book in which she'd first read about voodoo and looked through it for a section on reversing spells. She skimmed every page but found nothing. *I'll just have to make it up as I go along.*

Jessica cradled the voodoo doll in her arms like

a baby. She brought out the bowl of healing potion she had made for Benjamin and laid the Steven doll out on her bed. She took her lucky rabbit's foot and spread the healing potion all over the doll's body. It was a little messy, but if it worked for Benjamin, it might just work for Steven.

"Let my voodoo be undone. Let my voodoo be undone," she repeated over and over again.

Elizabeth walked into Jessica's room through the bathroom while Jessica was in the middle of her chanting.

"What are you doing? I thought you were done with your voodoo!" Elizabeth exclaimed.

"Keep your voice down," Jessica said. "I'm trying to reverse what I've done to Steven. I just hope it isn't too late. Do you think it will work?"

Elizabeth paused. "Look, Jess," she said finally, "I never believed this voodoo stuff at all, so I don't believe that it can be reversed. I really don't think you should worry about Steven."

Jessica shook her head. Poor Elizabeth had no idea how serious this was. *Maybe it's just as well that she doesn't really understand*, Jessica thought sadly. *She'll know soon enough.*

"Aren't you cooking tonight with Todd?" Jessica asked Elizabeth while she watched her sister make herself a sandwich in the kitchen that evening.

"Tonight's the night. Our project is due tomorrow, remember? Mom and Dad are going out, so we'll have the kitchen to ourselves," Elizabeth said.

"Did you change all the things around, like we talked about?" Jessica asked.

"I did exactly what you said. I put spices in different containers and I switched the salt and the sugar, since he always mixes those up. Oh, and I changed the tablespoons to teaspoons. He's terrible with measuring," Elizabeth said.

"How did you change the spoons?" Jessica asked, trying to follow the conversation. She was hoping to get her mind off Steven for a little while.

"I just stuck a piece of masking tape on the handle and wrote on them with a pen. I also changed the markings on the measuring cups. I think I've thought everything through perfectly. I've tried to remember every mistake he's made." Elizabeth took a deep breath. "I just hope he makes his usual mistakes."

"I'm sure he will," Jessica said confidently.

Jessica went into Steven's room later that evening to see if her healing voodoo had worked. Steven was lying on his bed, with his eyes open, looking pale and lifeless.

"Hi, Steven," Jessica said timidly. "How are you feeling?"

"Oh, hello, Jessica. How nice to see you," he said weakly.

How nice to see me? How nice to see your torturer? Jessica couldn't help thinking. Suddenly, looking at him lying there, she was overwhelmed with that horrible emotion that she very rarely felt: guilt.

"How are you feeling?" Jessica asked again.

"Pretty lousy, to tell you the truth," Steven said. "But don't worry about me. I don't want you to be bothered by my problems," he added dramatically.

"You're not bothering me," Jessica squeaked on the verge of tears. "Is there something I can get for you? Do you want a peanut butter sandwich or something?"

"No, that's OK. I'm really not hungry," he answered in a feeble voice.

Not hungry? Steven's always hungry, Jessica thought worriedly.

Steven gave a little cough. "Thanks for the kind offer, though."

Why did he have to be so nice to her? She couldn't stand it. It would be so much easier if he were being his usual obnoxious self.

Yes, guilt. That was what she was feeling. And it was the worst feeling in the world.

"This is going to be the best antebellum meal anyone's ever eaten west of the Mississippi," Todd said as he measured the flour carefully into the measuring cups.

Elizabeth was getting a little confused by all the changing around she did before. *Is that the flour or the powdered sugar?* she wondered.

"I've been going over these recipes again and

again and I practically have them memorized," Todd said. "You know, I was thinking of opening a restaurant out here in a couple of years. Something that specializes in Southern cuisine."

Elizabeth just offered a meek "terrific" and an "uh-huh." She was focusing on Todd's every move, trying to calculate if his mistakes would be rectified by her having moved things around. *Is he making his regular mistakes?* She was absolutely confused.

Why did I listen to Jessica? she wondered unhappily. *You would think I would have learned by now never to listen to any of her schemes.*

By the end of the evening, the Wakefields' kitchen was in complete disarray once again. Pots and pans were spilling out of the sink, and flour and cornmeal were all over the floors and counters.

"Well, I think this actually looks good enough to eat," Elizabeth said as she surveyed all the dishes they had prepared, lined up on the kitchen table.

"Of course it looks good enough to eat. It looks wonderful to eat, as a matter of fact. Why do you seem so surprised?" Todd asked.

"I have to admit, I was a little nervous," Elizabeth said. "Do you think we should maybe just take a little bite of everything to see how it tastes?"

"We'll ruin the presentation if we do that," Todd argued. "And besides, it will be more fun to taste everything tomorrow with the rest of the class. We don't want to ruin the surprise."

Elizabeth took another look at everything and

decided that it all looked the way it was supposed to. The corn bread and hush puppies seemed to be the right color and shape and the black-eyed peas looked perfect. The fish gumbo looked OK, although Elizabeth didn't really know what it was supposed to look like, since she'd never had it before.

There's nothing we can do about it now, Elizabeth thought to herself. *We'll just have to hope it tastes as good as it looks.*

Twelve

"Attention! Attention!" Todd said to Mrs. Arnette's social studies class the next morning. "Step right up for the best antebellum meal you've ever had in your life."

Elizabeth was mortified. Not only was she nervous about how the meal would turn out, she was embarrassed by the silly entertainer voice Todd was using in front of everyone.

"I think we should all give Todd and Elizabeth a big round of applause for cooking this beautiful meal for us," Mrs. Arnette said.

Unlike Jessica, who loved being the center of attention, Elizabeth was uncomfortable in the limelight. And she was so unsure about how the meal was going to taste that she would have preferred to hear the applause *after* everyone had eaten.

The students went up to the front of the room to pile up their plates and bowls with fish gumbo, hush puppies, corn bread, black-eyed peas, and peach cobbler. Elizabeth stood motionless at the back of the class waiting for their reactions.

Everyone sat back down at their desks and dug into their food. Time seemed to stand still as she stared into her classmates faces for some sign.

Suddenly Patrick Morris's face crumpled. Maria Slater's eyebrows shot up. Sarah Thomas started coughing.

"Water!" Melissa McCormick shouted.

Elizabeth watched in horror as almost every student started gagging! Anna Reynolds was spitting food into her napkin. Ellen Riteman's face had turned bright red.

Elizabeth turned to Mrs. Arnette in horror. She was sitting at her desk in the front of the chewing slowly on a bite of gumbo. Elizabeth watched the teacher's eyes widen and her face turn red. Mrs. Arnette covered her mouth and ran out of the room.

Oh, no! Elizabeth thought.

The room exploded into chaos and noise. Students were running around, gulping down glasses of water, shouting and coughing. Others were laughing hysterically at Mrs. Arnette.

Elizabeth put her head in her hands. She couldn't bear to look at Todd. *Oh, no.*

"Uh . . . excuse me, class?" Mr. Clark, the principal of the middle school, was standing in front of Mrs. Arnette's class looking uncomfortable. "Class, may I please have your attention? In light of this . . . uh . . . unusual situation, I'm dismissing this class early. Mrs. Arnette is not feeling well, but she'll be back tomorrow. You may all be excused."

Elizabeth's face was hot and she felt her eyes fill with tears.

Todd walked up to her also looking as if he was about to burst into tears. "I can't understand it," he said. "I knew those recipes backwards and forwards. I followed each instruction down to every last detail. What could have gone wrong?"

This is all my fault, Elizabeth thought woefully. *Todd must have done everything exactly right. I didn't trust him, and now I've ruined everything.*

Jessica walked over to Elizabeth and put her hand on Elizabeth's shoulder.

"Don't worry, Lizzie," Jessica said. "This kind of thing could happen to anyone. It was a major undertaking to cook for so many people."

Elizabeth shot her sister a look of irritation. *If I hadn't listened to you, this would never have happened,* she fumed silently. But she knew she shouldn't be mad at Jessica. Jessica had just been trying to help. The truth was, it was her fault for doing what Jessica suggested. It was a stupid idea, but it was even more stupid to have actually carried it out.

Elizabeth thought she was going to start crying, and that was something she didn't want to happen in front of the class. "Poor Todd," she said, trying to keep her voice even. "He was so excited about this project, and I just humiliated him in front of everyone."

"Everyone will forget about it by tomorrow. And besides"—Jessica gave her sister a lopsided grin—"it was pretty hilarious watching The Hairnet tear out of the room."

Elizabeth didn't see the humor in it at all. *I just hope Todd will still talk to me if he finds out what really happened,* she was thinking. She knew she should tell Todd what she'd done. It would make him feel better about himself. But on the other hand, it would make him furious at her.

Jessica brought the Steven doll into her bed that night and sang it a lullaby their mother used to sing to them when they were little. She made sure the little doll was warm and comfortable. She even rubbed off a couple of its pimples.

What if I actually kill Steven? she couldn't help worrying. *Mom and Dad would be so mad. They would never forgive me.* Jessica felt her eyes fill with tears. *Even though he teases me sometimes, he's the only brother I have. I don't want him to die. I love him.*

Jessica tossed and turned for what seemed like hours before she finally fell asleep.

Jessica was on the stage in the school auditorium. She was tied up to a pole, and smoke was at her feet. Steven's ghost was standing next to her, and it kept yelling, "Jessica Wakefield is an evil voodoo witch!"

Jessica looked out into the front row of the audience and saw all the Unicorns, Aaron Dallas, Bruce Patman, Elizabeth, and her parents. They were all yelling, "Voodoo witch! Voodoo witch!"

The flames from the fire were getting closer to Jessica. In a state of terror she felt the heat rise up her body.

Jessica woke up in a panic. Was that smoke she smelled? She ran into the bathroom to get a glass of water and saw something frightening: the Steven doll was lying in the sink, face down in a pool of water!

Oh, my God! What's going on? Jessica knew she hadn't put the doll there. Who had? She'd totally lost control of her powers. The voodoo had taken over, and poor Steven was a goner for sure!

Jessica raced down the hall and she felt her heart beating harder than ever before. She ran into Steven's bedroom screaming, "Steven! Steven!"

She pulled up short at his bed and put her hand on his shoulder. "Steven?" She couldn't tell if he was breathing or not because he was lying face down. She tried shaking him but he just kept lying motionless.

That's it! I've done it! I've killed him!

"Mom! Dad! Wake up!" Jessica shouted, tearing

down the hall and into her parents' bedroom. "I've killed Steven! Come quick!"

"What time is it?" Mr. Wakefield said as he sat up in bed and rubbed his eyes.

"Quick! We have to take him to a hospital! It might already be too late! It's all my fault!" Jessica was so upset that she was heaving and sobbing between her words.

Mrs. Wakefield sat up and tried to open her eyes. "Slow down, honey. Take a deep breath and tell us what's going on," she said calmly.

"It all started when Steven ruined my Johnny Buck poster and I was reading about voodoo in school and so I made this voodoo doll of Steven and I did awful things to it," she said in a rush, waving the doll around in the air to show as proof.

"I poked it with pens and pencils and forks and I spun it around and made it dizzy and I dropped food all over it at the kitchen table and at Casey's. I'm just the most terrible, awful person in the world," she finished with a sob. "Now, come *quick*, OK?"

Mr. and Mrs. Wakefield looked at each other with the usual expression they got when Jessica had gotten herself into a mess.

"I'm sure he's OK, but we'll go take a look at him to make you feel better," Mr. Wakefield said.

Jessica's parents got out of bed and put on their robes, which seemed to Jessica to take forever.

"What's going on in here?" Elizabeth asked, as

she walked sleepily into her parents' room. "What are you yelling about, Jess?"

"It's Steven," Jessica said breathlessly. "I think I killed him."

Elizabeth looked at her in surprise and followed Jessica and her parents down the hall to Steven's room.

Steven was now lying on his back. His eyes were rolled back into his head, there was saliva coming out of his mouth, and he didn't seem to be breathing at all.

All of the Wakefields were standing around his bed, peering down at him. Jessica studied his face intently, praying for some movement, some sign of life.

Suddenly his mouth twitched.

"Steven?" she said.

Were his eyes fluttering?

Jessica's heart was in her mouth when she realized he was alive! He was OK! He was . . . laughing.

Wait a minute.

He was laughing hysterically.

At her.

Thirteen

After school the next day, Jessica and Elizabeth went to Casey's to drown their sorrows in hot fudge sundaes. Jessica was still in shock from Steven's prank the night before. She'd been so exhausted she'd overslept that morning and hadn't even gotten to explain to her parents or figure out for herself what had been going on. She was worried she was going to be in big trouble, and she wasn't so sure she wanted to find out.

Lila Fowler came bounding up to their table and plopped down.

"I heard that five people went home from school yesterday because of that meal in social studies class," Lila said excitedly. She gave Elizabeth an admiring glance. "That was a pretty cool joke you played on the class, Elizabeth. I never knew you were such a practical joker. I thought that was Jessica's role in your family."

Jessica and Elizabeth looked at each other with a look that said, *I wish she would go away.*

"It wasn't exactly intentional," Elizabeth confessed.

"You're so modest," Lila said. "You might as well take the credit for it. It was totally cool."

Just then Bruce Patman, Aaron Dallas, Janet Howell, and Ellen Riteman entered Casey's and came over to the twins' table.

"Way to go, Wakefield," Bruce said to Elizabeth.

Even though Bruce was the most popular guy at Sweet Valley Middle School, Elizabeth thought he was obnoxious. She didn't care if he thought she was cool.

"Way to go what?" Elizabeth asked.

"Everyone's talking about what you did in The Hairnet's class yesterday. I never knew you had it in you," Bruce said.

"You never knew I had what in me?" Elizabeth asked.

"You know, the cool side. The schemer side of your personality," Bruce said.

"My sister is not a schemer," Jessica said in Elizabeth's defense. "And she happens to be cool naturally. She doesn't have to try to be cool like some people do."

"What's that supposed to mean?" Bruce asked, annoyed.

"You know what it means," Jessica said.

Leave it to Jessica to come through for me, Elizabeth thought to herself. She was so grateful that Jessica would risk insulting Bruce Patman in front of everyone to stick up for her.

"It was pretty funny to see the expression on Mrs. Arnette's face when she took her first bite of that gumbo," Ellen said, laughing.

Elizabeth shook her head. This conversation was just making her feel worse. She wished that everyone would go away and leave her and Jessica in peace.

"We have to go," Jessica said, coming to the rescue. "Elizabeth and I have somewhere we have to be."

Jessica and Elizabeth decided to stop by the day-care center and check on Benjamin before they went home. It was Jessica's idea. She was determined to prove that her voodoo had worked after all.

They walked out to the backyard of the center, where all the kids were running around, playing freeze tag. Jessica was absolutely ecstatic when she saw Benjamin running around with the rest of the boys and girls.

"Look at that!" Jessica squealed. "Look at Benjamin! He looks just like all the other kids. Hey, Benjamin! Hi!" she yelled across the playground.

Benjamin came running up to Elizabeth and Jessica with a big smile on his face. "Hi!" he said excitedly.

"You look terrific," Jessica said, beaming. "It's great to see you running around. How's your leg?"

"It's so much better," Benjamin said. "The pain has totally gone away. It's the best thing in the whole wide world that could have happened."

"Does the doctor know why it went away? Is it because of some new drug or something?" Elizabeth asked.

Jessica knew her sister well enough to know that she was asking that because she didn't want Jessica to think it had anything to do with her voodoo. *I don't care what she thinks*, Jessica said to herself. *I know it's because of me that he's better.*

"Actually, it's weird. The doctor isn't sure why it's better. The pain is even gone in the morning now. It's gone all the time! I think I'm totally cured," Benjamin said. "I don't even care why it's better. I'm just glad I can run around again like everyone else."

Jessica looked over at Elizabeth. She could tell that Elizabeth was frustrated by Benjamin's answer. *This just proves that I really do have healing powers*, Jessica thought. *Maybe I'm a voodoo witch after all.* Maybe instead of an evil witch, she was a good witch, like Glenda in the *Wizard of Oz*.

Jessica threw her arms around Benjamin and gave him a big hug.

"What was that for?" Benjamin asked, confused.

"Oh, nothing, really. You just proved something, that's all," Jessica said. "And I'm glad your leg's better."

"I hope you don't think that proved anything

about your voodoo powers," Elizabeth said to Jessica after Benjamin went back to his game of tag.

"What do you mean?" Jessica asked innocently.

"You know exactly what I mean," Elizabeth said.

"Oh, of course not," Jessica lied. "I'm sure there's a good medical explanation for Benjamin's recovery."

Elizabeth dropped Jessica off at home and decided to stop by Todd's house. Her stomach was tied up in knots as she imagined what he'd say when she explained the cooking fiasco. But she knew it was the right thing to do.

She rang the Wilkinses' doorbell and waited for what seemed to be an eternity for Todd to open the door. When he finally did, he only opened it partway and stood inside. He looked incredibly unhappy.

"Hi," Elizabeth said in almost a whisper. "Can you come outside and talk to me for a minute?"

"Look, I really don't feel like talking right now. I'm really sorry about what happened yesterday. I know it was all my fault. I'll tell the class that tomorrow if you want me to. But right now I think I want to be alone," Todd said.

Elizabeth felt guiltier than ever. She had no choice but to tell him the truth. "Todd, please just come outside. There's something really important I need to tell you," she pleaded.

Reluctantly, Todd walked outside and sat down

on the front steps of his house with Elizabeth.

"If you want to tell me that you never want to see me again," Todd said sadly, "I'll totally understand. I know that you're probably furious at me, and you have every reason to be. You don't have to say anything. I know what you're going to say. You always do great in all your classes, and now we'll probably both get a lousy grade in social studies class because of this. Maybe if I go in tomorrow and try to explain to Mrs. Arnette that it was all my fault, she won't punish you with a bad grade."

"Todd, listen, there's something you need to know," Elizabeth said in desperation.

"I don't know what happened," Todd said, interrupting Elizabeth. "I guess I just read the recipes wrong or something. I should just stick to basketball. That's really what I'm good at. I had a crazy idea that I could be a great chef. Boy, was I wrong. What an idiot."

"No, stop it!" Elizabeth was completely exasperated at this point. "Just listen to me for a minute. It was all my fault."

"Don't be silly," Todd said.

"Please let me talk for a while and don't say anything," Elizabeth begged. "*I* am totally responsible for what happened. I was afraid that you might mess everything up, since you hadn't cooked much before, so I did something absolutely unfair and wrong."

"What did you do?" Todd asked.

"I changed everything around. I tried to figure out what kinds of mistakes you usually make and I tried to out-mistake you," Elizabeth said.

"What do you mean? What did you change around?" Todd asked.

"I switched the salt and the sugar, for one thing. And I relabled some of the ingredients. I also changed the markings on the measuring cups and spoons," Elizabeth said. She was so nervous that her voice was shaking.

Todd sat absolutely still. For several moments he didn't say a word. Finally, his face broke into an enormous smile and he started laughing!

Elizabeth was completely baffled. *What could possibly be funny about what I just told him? Maybe he's so upset that he's gone into some kind of strange hysterical state!*

"Todd, are you OK?" Elizabeth asked.

"I'm absolutely wonderful!" Todd exclaimed. "You have made me so happy, Elizabeth Wakefield!"

Elizabeth couldn't believe it when he grabbed her and gave her a hug! "Why are you so happy?" she asked. "I thought you would never want to talk to me again as long as you lived."

"I thought I was a complete failure. I felt terrible for messing it up for you. Now I know that it wasn't my fault. Maybe I'll become a chef after all. Who knows? Anything could happen," Todd said triumphantly.

"But aren't you mad that I doubted you so much?" Elizabeth asked.

"No, not really. I hope you'll be honest with me after this. But I understand that you did all that scheming because you were just afraid to tell me the truth—that you thought I was a terrible cook and that I'd probably ruin the meal," Todd said.

"You're the greatest, Todd Wilkins! When you open your Southern restaurant, I'll be your first customer," Elizabeth said with relief and joy.

"I'd be honored to have you as my first customer, but you'll have to promise me one thing," Todd said, trying to make a serious face.

"Anything at all. Just name it," Elizabeth said eagerly.

"If you come to my restaurant, you'll have to stay out of the kitchen," Todd teased.

"That's a promise!" Elizabeth said.

Fourteen

Dinner that night at the Wakefield house was absolutely silent.

"We're waiting for an explanation about what happened last night," Mr. Wakefield said finally. "Will somebody please say something?"

Elizabeth looked at Jessica. Jessica looked at Steven. Steven looked at Elizabeth.

"OK, I'll explain," Elizabeth said at last. "Jessica told me about the voodoo doll she made of Steven and I decided to tell Steven about it."

"But you promised me you wouldn't tell!" Jessica shrieked.

"I was crossing my toes," Elizabeth confessed.

"Why did you tell him?" Jessica asked.

"I thought it would be funny if you really thought your voodoo was working. You wanted it to work so badly. I just had no idea how far it would go and how seriously you were taking it," Elizabeth said.

"But it did work. How do you explain all the times Steven responded to my pokes and everything?" Jessica asked.

"Every time you did your voodoo, I saw you, and I acted out whatever you were doing to the doll," Steven said, trying not to laugh again.

"But there were times when you couldn't have seen me. Like when you were playing basketball with Joe in the driveway. How do you explain that?" Jessica asked.

"If you remember, you were hanging out the window with your little doll. I saw you, but you didn't see me seeing you," Steven said.

"But Joe told me how strange you'd been acting. He said you'd been acting like a zombie," Jessica protested.

"I told Joe what you were doing. He just played along with it," Steven said.

"Well, what about the times at the table here? I always kept my doll on my lap, out of sight," Jessica said.

"I knew when you were doing something. You were always moving your hands around under the table, so I just figured it out," Steven said, obviously pleased with himself.

"But what about the days you stayed home from school, and why have you been looking so pale and tired lately?" Jessica demanded. She was so desperate to prove that her voodoo had really worked that she just couldn't accept all Steven's explanations.

"Didn't Steven tell you? The doctor called us yesterday and told us that Steven has a mild case of the flu. That's why he hasn't been feeling himself lately," Mrs. Wakefield explained.

Steven smiled and gave a shrug. "Pretty convenient, huh?"

Jessica let out a deep breath. "So I guess that time at Casey's you saw what I was doing with the whipped cream," Jessica said, deflated.

"Yep. And the time you hid behind the tree and I did a handstand in front of Cathy. I saw you the whole time," Steven admitted.

Jessica was disappointed, but she was also relieved. At least she knew Steven was back to being his old self—obnoxious.

"Jessica, honey, what's wrong?" Mrs. Wakefield asked at breakfast the next morning.

Jessica looked as though she was about to burst into tears. She was supposed to go in front of her social studies class that day and make her presentation about voodoo. She had been planning to tell how she'd used voodoo against Steven. Now she would have to tell everyone that it didn't work after all. She would be humiliated in front of all her classmates, and Mrs. Arnette, who was always assuming the worst about Jessica, would give her an

F. She had really hoped to get an A on her project and prove Mrs. Arnette wrong.

"I'm OK," Jessica lied. "Maybe I have Steven's flu."

"Do you want to stay home from school today?" Mr. Wakefield asked. "Do you think you have a fever?"

"I don't know. I have to go to school, though. Today is the day I'm supposed to make my social studies presentation," Jessica said sadly.

"Well, it can't possibly go any worse than mine did," Elizabeth said, trying to make Jessica feel better.

"News about that meal even got to Sweet Valley High. Everyone was saying how cool it was," Steven said as he piled four waffles onto his plate.

"I didn't think it was cool at all," Elizabeth said. "It was humiliating. I just hope I don't get a terrible grade because of it."

"You always get straight A's in that class. I wouldn't worry," Mrs. Wakefield said.

"Jessica, what is your social studies project? What kind of presentation are you making today?" Mr. Wakefield asked.

"I don't want to talk about it," Jessica said quietly. She thought she would start crying if she had to talk about it in front of Steven. She knew how much pleasure he would get out of ruining her school project.

"Please tell us. We'd like to know what you've been working on," Mrs. Wakefield pressed gently.

"Oh, OK," Jessica said reluctantly. "I was going to tell the class about voodoo."

Nobody said a word. They all looked at one an-other in surprise and sympathy—except for Steven, who burst out laughing.

"Jessica Wakefield, the voodoo witch!" Steven teased. "Watch out for her little magic doll. You never know if the doll is you."

Jessica's eyes filled with tears. "It's not funny, Steven. It's all your fault. You made me think my voodoo was working. And not only that, you really scared me. Now I have to get up in front of every-one and tell them that I'm a failure." Jessica's voice was shaking and she couldn't look at anyone. She just stared down at the untouched waffle on her plate.

"Steven, Jessica's right about that. It was cruel to let her think she was really hurting you," Mr. Wakefield said.

"That's my fault, too," Elizabeth admitted. "I was responsible for that as much as Steven. I'm sorry, Jess."

"I'm sorry, too," Steven mumbled.

"I don't think Jessica gets off so easily either," Mrs. Wakefield said. "You may get mad at your brother sometimes, but trying to hurt him like that is not the way to solve anything. In fact, it's the worst way to handle things."

"But it turns out that I *wasn't* hurting him at *all*," Jessica cried.

"You thought you were," Mr. Wakefield said. "That's just as bad as actually doing it."

"I do feel bad about scaring you so much," Steven said. "I realize that I went too far."

"You do?" Jessica asked in disbelief.

"So can we all agree that there will never be any more voodoo in our house?" Mr. Wakefield asked. "All those in favor say 'aye.'"

"Aye!" All the Wakefields said in unison. Jessica crossed her toes under the table. She couldn't break her own little personal rule of never saying never.

Just then, Steven did something that totally amazed Jessica and the whole family. He pulled out a long tube from under the table and handed it to Jessica.

"Here," he said. "I hope this will make up for the scare I gave you. I still think Johnny Buck is a bad singer and actor, but I guess you can get all gooey over him if you want."

Jessica pulled out a brand new poster of Johnny Buck that was exactly like the one Steven had ruined.

"Thank you! Thank you! Thank you!" Jessica exclaimed excitedly. "This definitely makes up for it, although—" Jessica paused for a minute and made a sweet, innocent face. "There is one teeny-weeny little thing you could still do."

"And what would that be?" Steven asked skeptically.

"Before you say no, just think about it for a minute. It's something you would totally get a kick out of," Jessica said, giving him her most charming smile.

"I'm afraid to ask," Steven said.

"Does it have anything to do with voodoo by any chance?" Mr. Wakefield asked suspiciously.

"Well, as a matter of fact," Jessica started. "It does have just a little bit to do with voodoo."

"Didn't we just make a decision to ban all voodoo?" Mrs. Wakefield asked with a smile.

"After today, the word *voodoo* won't come out of my mouth," Jessica said.

"OK, what's this thing you want me to do?" Steven asked once their parents had left the breakfast table to get ready for work.

"I want you to come to my class today and tell everyone how my voodoo worked," Jessica blurted out.

"But it *didn't* work," Elizabeth pointed out.

"Nobody really has to know that," Jessica said.

"So you're going to lie in front of Mrs. Arnette and our entire class?" Elizabeth asked.

"It's not exactly *lying*," Jessica said, taking an enormous bite of waffle. Suddenly her appetite was back. She always got incredibly hungry when she got excited. "*I* thought it was working, so in theory, it did kind of work."

"And what exactly are you and Steven going to do in class?" Elizabeth asked. She put her hands over her waffles to protect them from Jessica's fork.

"Well, I thought I would bring in the doll and I would explain all the different things I did to

Steven over the last week or so. Then I thought maybe I could blindfold him while I did different things to the doll and he would act it out," she explained. She reached her fork toward Elizabeth's plate, but Elizabeth cut it off with her own.

"But how will I know what you're doing?" Steven asked.

"We'll work out a code. That's where Elizabeth comes in," Jessica said.

"Did I just hear what I thought I heard?" Elizabeth asked, wrinkling her nose.

"Just come out with it," Steven said, exasperated.

"It's really very simple. Elizabeth will be in charge of signaling what kind of reaction you're supposed to be having. For example, if I'm poking the doll in the stomach, Elizabeth will cough once. If I'm poking you in the leg, Elizabeth will cough twice. If I'm poking you in the foot, Elizabeth will cough three times—" Jessica was totally wound up with excitement as she explained her plan.

"How do you suggest I get out of my own class at school?" Steven asked.

"You mean you're actually considering this?" Elizabeth asked in disbelief.

"It does sort of appeal to my sense of humor. And besides, I think I owe it to Jessica after all I put her through," Steven said.

"You're the best brother in the world!" Jessica exclaimed. "And don't worry about getting out of class. I can take care of that in a jiffy."

"How will you do that?" Elizabeth asked.

"It's simple. I'll just write a note saying you have a doctor's appointment," she said to Steven. "You already missed a couple of days of school this week because you were sick, so it will be totally believable."

"But why would they accept an excuse from you?" Elizabeth asked.

"It won't be from me. It will be from Mom," Jessica said as she managed to steal a bite of Elizabeth's waffle.

"But Mom's already gone to work," Elizabeth said.

Elizabeth really is slow sometimes, Jessica thought. *She has no sense of adventure.*

"I'll write the note. I've done it before. I can do Mom's signature exactly," Jessica said.

"Mom would be furious if she found out," Elizabeth cautioned.

"She won't find out," Jessica said confidently.

"I don't know about all this," Steven said wearily. "Maybe it's not such a good idea after all."

"Oh, please, please, please," Jessica begged. "Don't change your mind. It'll be fun."

"What will you do for me?" Steven asked.

"Anything at all," Jessica said.

"I get total power over the remote control for a month," Steven said.

"A whole month?" Jessica asked.

"One month—or no voodoo demonstration," Steven said resolutely.

"OK, it's a deal," Jessica conceded.

"Hey, no fair," Elizabeth protested. "This will affect me, too."

"Please, Lizzie," Jessica pleaded in the sweetest voice she could manage. "Just do this one little thing for me. I promise I'll somehow make it up to you."

"Will you explain to Todd that the whole cooking scheme was your idea?" Elizabeth asked.

"It's a deal," Jessica said triumphantly. "Now, let's take this voodoo show on the road!"

Fifteen

◇

"May I please have your undivided attention?" Mrs. Arnette said to her social studies class at the beginning of the period. "Today we have a special visitor from Sweet Valley High. Steven Wakefield, Jessica and Elizabeth's brother and my old student, is here to help Jessica with her project. I'm not sure what they have planned for us, but I'm sure it will be interesting."

You'll definitely find it interesting, Jessica thought excitedly, walking with Steven to the front of the room. She held up her Steven doll for all to see.

"I'm going to talk about voodoo," Jessica began. She loved speaking in front of the class. Unlike most people, she never got nervous when the attention was on her. Today she spoke loudly and confidently.

"A couple of weeks ago," she continued, "I made this voodoo doll to look just like my brother, Steven. I did different little things to torture the doll, and my brother responded to everything I did."

"Is that true, Steven?" Mrs. Arnette asked skeptically.

"Oh, absolutely," Steven responded.

"May I continue?" Jessica asked, trying to sound annoyed by the interruption.

"Go on," Mrs. Arnette said.

"One time, I poked the doll in the stomach and I watched while the real Steven grabbed his stomach and doubled over in pain," Jessica said proudly.

"If you saw him, how do you know he didn't see you?" Caroline asked.

Leave it to Miss Busybody-Caroline to try to trip me up, Jessica thought. "He didn't see me because I was hidden behind the door," Jessica said. "If you don't believe me, why don't you ask Steven?"

"Is that true, Steven?" Caroline asked.

"That's the absolute truth," Steven lied.

"If there are no more questions, I will continue with my presentation," Jessica said with a professional air. "Another time, I poked the Steven doll in the feet and the real Steven started hopping around the room."

There were murmurs of "wow" and "cool" in the classroom, which served to propel Jessica on with her story.

"On a separate occasion I dripped milk onto the doll's shirt." Jessica was walking around the front of the classroom and talking like one of the lawyers on her favorite soap opera. "You can imagine my surprise when I saw my very own brother spill milk on himself at the exact same moment."

The reactions around the room became louder and more excited. Jessica was thrilled.

"Now, I would like to do a demonstration, if I may. Steven, please sit down on this chair," Jessica commanded, pointing to a chair in the front of the class. She tied a red bandanna around his eyes. "Steven will sit here blindfolded while I stand over here with the voodoo doll. You will observe that his reactions will correspond to my exact movements."

Jessica moved a couple of yards away from Steven and looked at Elizabeth, who was seated in the front row. Jessica held up a long knitting needle and poked the doll in the stomach. At first there was silence throughout the room. Jessica shot an urgent look at Elizabeth. Finally, after what seemed an eternity, Elizabeth coughed once.

Steven grabbed his stomach dramatically and bent over in his chair. The whole class broke into applause.

"Now, for demonstration number two," Jessica said. She could almost imagine a drum roll in her head. Slowly, Jessica moved the needle toward the doll and poked it in the leg.

Please remember the code, Lizzie. Don't let me down, Jessica was thinking.

To Jessica's delight, Elizabeth coughed twice. Jessica looked over at Steven, who grabbed his leg suddenly. "Ouch!"

Jessica poked the foot of the doll, and Elizabeth coughed three times. This time, Steven grabbed his foot and rolled off the chair and onto the floor.

The classroom was filled with thunderous applause and laughter.

Although she was pleased by the class response, Jessica was slightly irritated at Steven's overly dramatic reaction. She was afraid people might suspect it was a setup if he overdid it.

"Are you all right?" Mrs. Arnette asked, looking at Steven on the floor.

The Hairnet bought it—hook, line, and sinker, Jessica thought excitedly.

"I'm OK," Steven said, sitting up on the floor. He rubbed his foot as if it were hurting him.

"I think this has been quite enough for now," Mrs. Arnette said in a huff. She helped Steven back onto the chair and untied the bandanna. "Steven, I think you should return to Sweet Valley High—and class, I think you should turn to page fifty-six of your textbooks."

"Thanks a million," Jessica whispered to Elizabeth when she sat back down next to her. She slapped Steven on the hand as he walked by her on his way out.

"Jessica," Mrs. Arnette said when the bell rang

at the end of class. "I'd like to see you for a moment, please."

"Yes?" Jessica asked innocently as she approached the desk.

"I don't know what happened in my classroom today," Mrs. Arnette said, shaking her head. "But I don't like it, and I know our principal and the parents of the students in this school won't like it either. Now, I do not believe in voodoo and I don't believe that what you did today was voodoo."

"But—"

Mrs. Arnette held up her hand. "I do, however, feel that your project represented a great deal of effort, and for that reason you are to be graded accordingly . . ."

A! Jessica was thinking excitedly. *A, A, A!*

"Which means I'll give you a . . . C plus."

"Oh."

"I was pleased to see you show so much enthusiasm about something in this class for a change. But I don't want you to mention the word 'voodoo' to any Sweet Valley student ever again and I don't want you to practice any voodoo ever again. Is that understood?"

Jessica nodded. "My voodoo days are over."

Jessica's voodoo presentation was the main topic of discussion throughout the cafeteria that day. Jessica was loving the attention as students were crowding around the Unicorner to ask her about voodoo.

"It's really a power one is born with," Jessica was saying to the group. "I've known for most of my life that I've had these magic abilities, but I don't like to abuse them."

"Do you think you could help me make a voodoo doll of my brother, Joe? He's really been getting on my nerves lately. I'd love to give him a few good pokes every now and then when he's really bugging me," Janet said.

"Oh, sure. I could probably help you out with that," Jessica said.

"I was wondering if you could make a bunch of voodoo dolls of our rival basketball teams," Ken Matthews said. "Before the games, you could break all the dolls' legs."

"That could work," Jessica said. "I'd never considered doing a whole group of dolls at the same time before."

"Oh, Jessica," Elizabeth called as she peered into the group surrounding her sister's table. "Can I see you for a moment please?"

"I'm kind of busy now," Jessica said. She hated to leave when she was getting so much attention.

"Jessica," Elizabeth said again, this time more sternly than the first. "I need to talk to you *now*."

Jessica got up from the table and followed Elizabeth over to a table that was empty.

"What's up?" Jessica asked distractedly. "There

are a lot of people waiting to talk to me, Lizzie, so could you maybe just say whatever it is you wanted to talk about?"

Elizabeth rolled her eyes and sighed deeply. "Jessica, look at me," she said urgently.

"Why do you have such a serious face?" Jessica asked.

"Don't you remember what Mom and Dad said this morning about voodoo?" Elizabeth asked.

"Yes. So?"

"And don't you remember what you told me Mrs. Arnette said to you this morning?"

"Yes. So?" Jessica said again.

"Well?" Elizabeth was totally frustrated. "What do you think you're doing over there?"

"I'm just answering questions. Everyone's curious about my special powers," Jessica said.

"First of all, you don't *have* any special powers. And secondly, I think you should just stop talking about it. The parents of all these people wouldn't exactly be thrilled if their kids came home and started making voodoo dolls. And if *our* parents found out you were responsible, they would be absolutely furious," Elizabeth said.

"You sound exactly like Mrs. Arnette," Jessica pouted. "You take the fun out of everything."

"Promise you'll stop it?"

"Yes, I'll stop it," Jessica said.

"Oh, and another thing—"

"Enough lectures, already," Jessica said.

"I'm not going to give a lecture. But there is one thing you forgot to do." Elizabeth looked over at Todd who was sitting at a table across the room.

"Oh—Todd," Jessica said. "I almost forgot. I'll be right back."

Jessica walked over to the table where Todd was sitting and plopped down next to him. "Hey, Todd, can I talk to you for a minute?"

"Sure. That was a great presentation you did in class today," Todd said as he put down the sandwich he was eating and wiped off his mouth. "It was a whole lot better than mine and Elizabeth's."

"That's what I wanted to talk to you about," Jessica said.

"What? Voodoo? I don't really know that much about it," Todd said.

"No, I wanted to talk to you about your cooking project," Jessica said.

"That's one thing I'd rather forget about, to tell you the truth," Todd said, looking down at his plate.

"I just wanted to let you know that all that scheming Elizabeth did was my idea," Jessica confessed.

"You really don't have to cover for Elizabeth. She told me all about it and I wasn't mad at all. In fact, I was totally relieved."

"Well, I'm glad you're not mad, but it really is true. Elizabeth is good at a lot of things but trouble-making isn't one of them. That's my department," Jessica said.

Todd just looked at her and laughed. "Thanks for telling me, Jess."

"This fried chicken is delicious," Mr. Wakefield said as he reached for another big piece at the dinner table that night.

"The biscuits melt in your mouth. This was really nice of you two to make dinner for us tonight," Mrs. Wakefield said to Todd and Elizabeth.

"It was Todd's idea," Elizabeth said, beaming.

"I thought it was the least we could do after you all had to suffer through our early efforts," Todd said, and bit into a biscuit.

"This time, Todd supervised *me*," Elizabeth said.

"Steven, this is for you," Jessica said as she handed him a box with a big, red bow tied around it.

"What's the occasion? It's not my birthday or anything," Steven said as he opened it. Steven pulled out a blue oxford shirt that was exactly like the one Jessica had ripped up.

"My lucky shirt! I was wondering where this was," Steven said.

"It's not the same one, Steven," Jessica confessed. "I hope it will still be lucky, though. I ripped up yours to make a shirt for my voodoo doll."

"Did you have to mention voodoo again after what happened today?" Steven said as he took a huge bite of chicken.

"What do you mean by that?" Mr. Wakefield

asked suspiciously. "Did something happen today that we don't know about?"

Jessica looked at Elizabeth and Steven and gave them each a conspiratorial smile. "Nothing happened," Jessica said sweetly.

"Good. I was afraid you might have forgotten our agreement about this," Mr. Wakefield said.

"Nope," all three Wakefield kids said at the same time.

"Hey, thanks a lot for the new shirt, Jessica," Steven said.

"You're welcome." Jessica paused for a minute then added, "Steven, there is one thing I'd like to ask you to do."

"I thought I'd done enough favors for one day. What is it?" he asked.

"I think I'd like to have you go back to your teasing, obnoxious ways. I don't really recognize you when you're being so nice to me," Jessica said.

"It's a deal," Steven said. "I was getting pretty tired of being nice myself."

Jessica was getting books from her locker after homeroom the next morning when Aaron Dallas walked up.

"Hey, Jess," he said.

Jessica turned to look at him. A piece of hair on the top of his head was sticking straight up. *Why can't he brush his hair in the morning?* she wondered. It was hard to take him seriously when he had this thing sprouting out of his head.

"Hi, Aaron," she said, turning back to her locker.

"I just wanted to tell you, that was a really groovy presentation you did yesterday in The Hairnet's class," he said.

Groovy? Jessica's eyebrows shot up. *Who says groovy anymore?*

She stared at him as though she were looking at him for the first time. *He's really not as cute as I thought he was,* she thought unhappily. *And why does he say such dumb things sometimes?*

Suddenly Jessica had a terrible thought. *Maybe it really is over between Aaron and me. Maybe he isn't the guy of my dreams after all.*

What will happen when Jessica decides to find a new boyfriend? Find out in Sweet Valley Twins and Friends #79, Jessica's Blind Date.

SIGN UP FOR THE SWEET VALLEY HIGH® FAN CLUB!

Hey, girls! Get all the gossip on Sweet Valley High's® most popular teenagers when you join our fantastic Fan Club! As a member, you'll get all of this really cool stuff:

- Membership Card with your own personal Fan Club ID number
- A Sweet Valley High® Secret Treasure Box
- Sweet Valley High® Stationery
- Official Fan Club Pencil (for secret note writing!)
- Three Bookmarks
- A "Members Only" Door Hanger
- Two Skeins of J. & P. Coats® Embroidery Floss with flower barrette instruction leaflet
- Two editions of *The Oracle* newsletter
- Plus exclusive Sweet Valley High® product offers, special savings, contests, and much more!

Be the first to find out what Jessica & Elizabeth Wakefield are up to by joining the Sweet Valley High® Fan Club for the one-year membership fee of only $6.25 each for U.S. residents, $8.25 for Canadian residents (U.S. currency). Includes shipping & handling.

Send a check or money order (do not send cash) made payable to "Sweet Valley High® Fan Club" along with this form to:

SWEET VALLEY HIGH® FAN CLUB, BOX 3919-B, SCHAUMBURG, IL 60168-3919

NAME_____
(Please print clearly)

ADDRESS_____

CITY_____ STATE _____ ZIP_____
(Required)

AGE _____ BIRTHDAY_____ /_____ /_____